I0726921

The Lighthouse

The
Lighthouse

David Osborn

Published by Dagmar Miura
Los Angeles
www.dagmarmiura.com

The Lighthouse

Copyright © 2023 David Osborn
All rights reserved. No part of this book may be used or reproduced in any manner whatsoever without prior written permission except in the case of brief quotations embodied in critical articles or reviews. For information, address Dagmar Miura, dagmarmiura@gmail.com, or visit our website at www.dagmarmiura.com.

This is a work of fiction. Names, characters, businesses, places, events, and incidents are either the products of the author's imagination or used in a fictitious manner. Any resemblance to actual persons, living or dead, or actual events is purely coincidental.

cover image: composite including a photo by Joshua Hibbert via Unsplash

First published 2023

ISBN: 978-1-956744-87-3

To my family, with love

One

An immaculate black SUV pulled up to the curb on Main Street of the little village of Shinnecock, and its well-groomed driver, in a business suit complimented by a white shirt and necktie, got out. His wearing dark glasses on a gloomy sunless day was Angi's first indication that the president was in residence. The driver and car were United States Secret Service.

For many years, President Aaron Denver's large family summer home, the sprawling lawn and beach embracing the many-bedroom shingled house on Shinnecock Bay and known as The Dock, was only a short walking distance down the empty Atlantic coastline from the village of Shinnecock.

The one person, among the six hundred people of the village, who'd be most affected by the president taking up his usual summer month's residence at The Dock was Angela Cajun, Shinnecock's sole cop. Affectionately known to most as plain Angi, or more formally, the town cop, she was a young, attractively spirited, and athletic black woman, age twenty-six, and an active police officer for more than six years with the small fifty-man police force at Barthchester, a sizeable coastal town six miles distant and a summer resort with a popular beach, and the haven for ferries that went to offshore islands.

Seconded to work summertime in Shinnecock as the village's sole cop, Angi bore the burden during every year not just of the president's too often arrogant family and staff along with the Secret Service personnel and state troopers, but also of the small tidal wave of tourists wanting somehow to feel elevated by the presidential presence so close by.

Other than keeping village order during presidential visits, Angi's job was also to protect Shinnecock's famous lighthouse from tourists who, besides photographing every nook and cranny of the village along with its inhabitants, were especially drawn to insistently gawk, photograph, and constantly try to get to it.

For many years no longer in use, its light extinguished by modern times, the lighthouse was part of an historic trust established and owned by the Denver family. It stood just outside the village on a narrow point that was surrounded by sea on both sides, and it was Angi's job to visit it twice daily to make certain nobody had somehow slipped past her and get to it, or, when the president was in residence, managed to sneak past the Secret Service or state troopers protecting it from being a long-range viewing site for paparazzi or even used as a sniper's nest.

As town cop, Angi shared a tiny police station office in an alley back of Babcock's Pharmacy with Charley How, with Charley's desk in one corner and hers in the other taking up most of the room's limited space. A sign over the door said POLICE, and its prisoner lockup was nothing more than a storeroom with a built-in iron cot, a toilet, and an ordinary door for bars.

Gray-haired, balding, and a widower, Charley had served long years with the NYPD before retiring to Shinnecock when his wife inherited a family home just outside the village. Performing a small role in the village's police duties, he came three times a week every summer to keep an official record of whatever Angi reported as a breach of law and order.

Babcock's pharmacy was one of Shinnecock's few signs of commerce, along with Ginelli's grocery store, the one-teller branch of the Western National Bank, Paul's Pizza, the Cross Roads Hardware, and a tourist bureau that was open only in summertime. For anything of greater need, Shinnecock residents drove to Barthchester.

The lighthouse, well over two hundred years old, had been built to protect ships from foundering on dangerous hidden rocks known to mariners as The Shelf. It had been rescued from oblivion in the late 1900s when put up for sale by the government and bought with cash by Amos Denver, the oil baron grandfather of the current president. After seeing the lighthouse from the sea while on his yacht, Amos had come to the area with a suitcase full of money and had also bought with cash all the impoverished farms that lined the coast from the lighthouse to Barthchester. He had then built The Dock in shallow Shinnecock Bay and close to Shinnecock Village as a family summer residence.

A protected national monument still proudly overlooking the dangerous waters off Shinnecock Bay, the lighthouse's dominance belied the fact that bit by bit its solid rock masonry was aging. Tall and slender, its white exterior now showed occasional patches of weathered stone where its surface paint had peeled away, while the small stone keepers house attached to the very bottom looked battered by winter weather.

High above, nearly five stories up, a narrow steel catwalk encircling the top with a rail only waist high. It was dangerously rusted, and the band of windows circling ancient machinery operating its warning lights were dimmed by years of wind-blown salt spray.

Inside the lighthouse, once shiny mirrors reflecting the bright flames of a kerosene lamp flashed intermittent signals of bright light which could be seen for miles by ships at sea.

But if time had dimmed its warning light, its proud presence remained, year after year, to be regarded with near reverence by many who saw it.

Two

If the lighthouse inevitably attracted those with a consuming interest in historic relics, it was often seen differently and not always with pride but as something of a nuisance by many of the Shinnecock villagers. More than just a few wished it could be torn down and no longer an attraction that brought crowds of tourists to village streets during the warm months of summer, severely disrupting the privacy of its inhabitants. Shinnecock residents loved the peace and quiet that such an isolated village, nestled against the sea on a rocky coast, could provide. Many considered the presence of state troopers, along with personnel of the Secret Service whenever the president was in residence close by, as an effrontery, and bore it with resigned and sometimes barely concealed hostility.

In an even more unwanted downside, it also, in its isolation, attracted homeless men or drunks wanting to sleep off days of far too many, youthful lovers seeking privacy in their passion, rowdy teens who took delight in spray-paint vandalism, and other unwanteds who invariably left empty cans, bottles, and paper cups as well as used condoms lying about, along with other unsightly refuse to be cleaned up in the once-a-week visit of Shinnecock's one-man sanitation department.

Otherwise, only old Farney Gould, a rough and salty lobsterman who daily trolled for lobsters along The Shelf, was officially allowed at the lighthouse. Like his father and grandfather before him, Farney had lived in the little stone house perched on rocks at the base of the lighthouse almost from the day the Denver family had made the lighthouse a trust and established residence at The Dock. Once the abode of generations of the lighthouse's keepers, it safely stored his lobster traps and saved him from almost daily runs in his little lobster boat to the commercial market at Barthchester down the coast.

It was on such a day that Angi pushed impatiently from her desk and prepared to go to work when Charley muttered, "Big day, I hear." He was seated at his desk and hunched over a coffee, sleeves rolled up, and he barely looked up from sorting out the various warnings and tickets issued during the week by Angi for everything from traffic violations to litter.

And Angi said back, "Secret Service guy said

last night they're having a whole extra contingent coming in this morning."

"Oh? What's up?"

Angi shrugged. "Some kind of a big brouhaha at The Dock."

Wearing her usual nonuniform jeans and a well-worn blue work shirt, she slung her police utility belt around her hips, holstered Glock, taser, phone, and all, pinned her police badge high on the left breast of her shirt, and pushed away from her desk. "Helicopter coming in this afternoon."

"A helicopter ?" The news brough Charley's grizzled head up, and protest flickered in his old eyes as he understood what that meant. "Them," he muttered.

The one word, spoken with a touch of hostility, indicated his feelings toward the numerous Denver family and their servants along with the skeletal entourage of White House officialdom who always accompanied the president when he came to The Dock for his annual four-week vacation.

"Yeah," Angi said, with equal feeling. She hated presidential visits, with the unwanted presence of state troopers and the large Secret Service contingent all over the place and forever getting in the way. The visits also meant several added hours a day to her normal ten, and a forced neglect of other functions, like answering various complaints of one kind or another that always seemed to fall on her shoulders in the too often absence of Al George, the nominated village mayor, who invariably, when most needed, was away in Barthchester on what he declared "official business" but actually, Angi knew, was usually visiting his girlfriend of many years.

"So here we go again," she added, and left the office, with a casual "See ya" thrown at Charley, already engrossed in paperwork.

She had hardly emerged from the alley behind Babcock's pharmacy onto the open square beyond and then, walking down Main Street toward the sea, had reached the foot of the village, when she found her way toward the path which led to the lighthouse barred by one of the many Secret Service agents who now suddenly seemed everywhere. Parked SUVs dominated the village streets as well as identically suited agents, each wearing forever dark glasses so fixed to their expressionless faces that you could never clearly see what they were thinking, and making each seem like an alien from outer space.

The voice of the agent Angi found blocking her way was as anonymous as his appearance. "Sorry, lighthouse barred."

Angi wasted no word of politeness. She said with icy abruptness, "Hey. Go fuck yourself, big man, okay? This is my town. Not yours. I go where I want." And jabbing one finger at the badge she'd only just pinned on, she shoved past the startled agent who, caught off guard, failed to resist. It was ritual, a routine confrontation that Angi practiced every year when the president arrived, the Secret Service with him.

"Pays to get things right first day," she muttered to herself, before continuing to the lighthouse.

Three

Stephanie Crist dropped down onto the chair at the side of the tennis court with a sigh of relief. Tennis, often daily, was always a distraction from work as usual since she'd come to The Dock. And today she'd had to play especially early before work, began and even before much of the household was up.

In her late twenties, Stephanie was part of the very small skeletal Summer White House, which the president always brought along on his annual holiday. An intern, her boss was Robert Belknap, the deputy chief of staff who'd also come.

Stephanie hid her feelings as she had when carefully holding back in playing with Beth Harquist, the president's married daughter, whom she'd allowed to win. The same age as Stephanie,

Beth was a good enough tennis player, but not up to Stephanie's standards. At college, Stephanie had been on the varsity team at U Penn, where she had won flawless matches with an ability that had earned her a high standing in collegiate tennis, when she was seen in a close match in the semifinal round of a national tournament in Tucson.

Beth took the chair next to Stephanie, without comment wiping her face and bare shoulders with a towel readily supplied by a court attendant and feeling a glow of victory while oblivious that winning had been handed to her, or even that, simply as a matter of course, Stephanie's deferring to any of the president's family was a rule in the political game.

Both women were silent for a moment. A barrier of trees and a high wire fence separated the well-kept surface of the court from the gravel driveway that ended in a large oval before The Dock, the several stories of which rose commandingly, a classic of twentieth-century seaside exclusivity and wealth. The shingled charm of the house with its mansard rooftops obscured all of the ocean beyond, while just up the rocky shore, the towering lighthouse, along with the village of Shinnecock, served as a guardian border post to the sprawling lawns and gardens around the house.

Directly off the awning-shaded bay-side terrace of The Dock, a large swimming pool would soon be all-day-long host to the noisy flock of the president's grandchildren playing at water polo, the sport that had been intimately shared with the public through the endless photo publicity garnered by relentless paparazzi, who photographed when they could each and every one in the family.

A spacious lawn led from the pool to a small sandy beach that was a break in the rocky shore and where a short pier, extending out into Shinnecock Bay, ended with a float that was often used for adult swimming. A small dory was tethered to it to take the president and family out to the anchored sloop, *The Swallow,* for like his Grandfather Amos, President Aaron Denver loved sailing.

"Gosh, Steph." Beth Harquist finally spoke first. "That was close. You almost had my serve and the set with it."

Stephanie offered an obligatory laugh. "Watch out, Beth. One of these days I'm going to beat you hollow."

It was a pretense. Everything was a pretense. Pretense was the way it had to be with all of the president's children, as well as the president, and especially with his self-centered wife, Adrienne, to whom being first lady meant forever maintaining the immaculate never-aging appearance of the glamorous model she'd once been, while acting as though she'd personally won the perfect place in life for commanding universal high fashion.

Almost from her first day interning, Stephanie had learned that you yielded not just to the awesome power of the Oval Office but also to the extraordinary charisma and self-assurance that glowed first from the president then from his whole family as well, the famous Denver personality that had easily earned Aaron Denver his second term.

Besides Beth Harquist, who, along with her husband, a young political appointee given a position high up in the EPA, was staying at the dock, there were her two brothers, with their wives, the names of whom Stephanie kept forgetting and always at the most awkward moment. Each had produced what seemed a positive horde of Aaron Denver's progeny. Children of all ages rushed about everywhere, completely out of the control of uniformed nannies. The air both within and outside the house was constantly filled with their shrieking and shouting. Stephanie found it hard not to compare their innocent play to the truth about their elders to whom she had endlessly to kowtow: the reality of their parents' utter dysfunctional lives and secrets, so hidden from all but a bare handful.

Cheerfully agreeing to a return match with Beth, Stephanie left the young woman chatting with the nanny, who had appeared with Beth's toddler and her six-month-old just a little late to see their mother triumph over her tennis opponent. Crack-of-dawn tennis was okay, Stephanie thought, for the privileged, but for her it interfered with work and more work, and especially today, when she had defied all odds by agreeing to a very early, first-thing tennis match before the day really began.

She'd only done so because, along with anybody else who counted, she had been unexpectedly told late yesterday that there was to be a top-secret meeting early that afternoon when The Dock would see flown in, by Marine Corps helicopter, the Saudi Arabian foreign minister, the U.S. Secretary of State, Charles Sanctford, and Prince Ahmed Faisal bin Tala, representing the Saudi's supreme leader. The purpose of the meeting was to try urgently once more to negotiate the freedom of two American scientists seized while exploring desert botany and held hostage by the Saudis. Using the false charge of "espionage" as leverage, the Saudis were attempting to gain the release of one of their own embassy people in Washington, whom the FBI had arrested for an attempt to steal top-secret information on a nuclear armed drone recently developed by the Pentagon.

Four

Coming off the tennis court and gaining the air-conditioned sprawling sanctuary of The Dock, Stephanie first entered the welcome coolness of the large modern living room, its silence not yet broken as it soon would be by the shouts and cries of children at water polo in the pool beyond. Wasting no time even thinking about them or anything else except work, she went straight to a wing of the house added to accommodate the president's summer entourage and which had come to be known as the Summer White House.

Passing a small room occupied by a naval officer who caried "The Bomb," America's nuclear launch device, wherever the president went, she waved at Mara Harmon. An intense scholarly young woman who hid her thoughts behind oversize eyeglasses and whose dark hair always seemed tangled and uncared for, Mara was also an intern, sending "Summer White House" news to Alice Fogerty, the press secretary back in Washington. Journalist-trained, she had been a reporter with the *Portland Press Herald* in Maine. She and Stephanie shared a tiny attic bedroom while at The Dock.

Stephanie glanced only briefly into the adjoining room, where two technicians monitored a complex system of audio and video equipment. They provided instant communication between the president and the skeletal Summer White House with administration officials in Washington, making it seem to the president, whatever the moment, that he was actually still in the Oval Office.

Their job, especially today, Stephanie knew, was critical to the meeting, and they had already been working for hours. She herself had been kept busy with the visit until late yesterday evening, and she had already been to the office today before tennis and the rest of the work force had even had breakfast in order to get vital work done for the meeting. It was the only reason for her to so early oblige the President's tennis-crazy daughter, who'd play at any hour.

Stephanie went on to the third room occupied by herself and her boss, Robert Belknap, who was in hourly contact with the Oval Office back in Washington. Brought along for the month when the president was on vacation to assist whenever necessary, even to doing secretarial work, Stephanie's own desk was discreetly placed in a far corner. Although only an intern, her ability to handle complicated tasks, along with her air of confidence, had led more and more top executives at the White House to entrust her with privileged information, unusual for one so young. Although she did not have maximum security clearance, in the close and frantically busy atmosphere of the Oval Office and surrounding rooms, her presence was often carelessly taken for granted, and she continuously heard, casually and openly discussed, many aspects of administration work others were never party to.

Stephanie was not surprised to find Belknap on the phone reviewing specifics of the afternoon meeting with his boss, Hank Whittaker, the Chief Of Staff and real power in the Presidency. Yesterday, he had gone over every moment of the secret Saudi visit, and today was doing it yet again, and had canceled playing golf at Barthchester, where there was an eighteen-hole course.

"Where the hell have you been?" he demanded, putting down his secure cell phone on hearing her come in.

"Sorry, sir. Tennis. Beth Harquist."

"Bloody woman and her tennis," Belknap muttered. And then, "Just got a call from Hank. Saudis are coming by an hour earlier than planned. No reason why. This whole meeting is a farce. It's just Saudi PR. They have no intention of agreeing to try once more to negotiate release of the two scientists."

Wearing a sweatshirt rather than his

Washington uniform, a well-tailored business suit, white shirt, and tie, Belknap was in his late middle years, gray-haired, balding, and slightly overweight, as emphasized by his relatively short stature as well as by his lack of muscular development from never exercising and endlessly drinking too much at day's end.

Still hunched over his phone, protectively, as though someone might see some forbidden secret on it that he had to keep hidden, he said, "Family all set on the meeting?"

Stephanie said, "Yes, sir. The first lady's been informed. The rest all expect the day to be as usual." One reason Stephanie had been playing tennis was part of the need to maintain normalcy until the very last moment.

In the all too frequent need to say "yes" since she'd been assigned to assist Belknap, Stephanie discovered within herself a brewing dislike for the man who held enough political power to have achieved his position.

Robert Belknap was a narcissist, a bully who drank too much, and as far as Stephanie was concerned, something even worse. She found him inherently deceitful. He'd been plucked by President Denver from relative obscurity in the cutthroat world of the West Wing, where he'd established himself as a liaison officer to the Pentagon following a tour as a deputy AG with the Justice Department, all the while slyly hiding his inherent opposition to every constructive measure that was part of the president's agenda.

His wife, Cheryl, with whom he was rarely seen in public, appeared to Stephanie to be an intimate friend of the first lady, and was seen constantly in her company since both were at The Dock for the month. Stephanie often found herself wondering what the woman found in her husband. Cheryl Belknap was exceptionally pretty and, in direct contrast to him, cheerful and friendly with everyone, but in a way, Stephanie thought, that was superficially shallow, even false.

Stephanie heard Belknap say, "Inform the goons of the meeting if they don't already know," and knew he meant Secret Service agents, the hard-working group whose presence he often disparaged. She said, "Yes, sir. Of course. Although I suspect they have already heard from Washington. A whole new team of them came yesterday."

"You'll need to talk to all three of the children's nannies confidentially. But be careful. Only that there's a meeting. And a reception following."

"Yes, sir. I'll suggest that the grandchildren will be confined to the dining room. One of the nannies has experience as a part-time puppeteer, and she and the other two nannies can arrange a puppet show to keep the children quiet."

Belknap grunted. He wanted no problems. He said abruptly, "And Mara?"

"Miss Harmon will be covering, sir."

"Just remind her to keep her fucking activist mouth shut."

"She's aware of full secrecy, sir, believe me."

Stephanie kept to herself the ridiculousness of his thinking that Mara Harmon, of all people, would divulge the top secrecy of the meeting. Mara would be perhaps more critically aware of the need for silence than anybody. But for some illogical reason so typical of the White House, Belknap had long nurtured a dislike of her. Perhaps, Stephanie occasionally thought, he harbored secret anti-Semitism.

"Just make sure she gets the name of that asshole Saudi prince correctly in her file. Don't want any fuckups there. It's Ahmed Faisal bin Tala. Got that?"

Stephanie hid any reaction to Belknap's language. She'd become used to it. Just as she'd become used to his arrogance and hypocrisy. When first just down the hall from the Oval Office and, when doors were left open, she could often hear much of what the president said, she'd found herself wondering not only how Belknap had got the job, but how he managed to keep it. The answer lay, she realized, in his always being able to say what others wanted to hear—a norm, it seemed, in Washington. Or was it just politics as usual with any government, whether in Washington, Paris, Oslo, or Beijing? Few who spoke up honestly seemed to last.

She repeated the name of the Saudi leader's personal representative silently to herself to remember it, although she'd already carefully written it down. She said calmly, "Yes, sir."

"And we've got to make sure nothing's leaked

by Benji." This was the name all the family called Barijees Alama, the internationally famous Lebanese and the darling of the celebrity world, who'd been invited to stay at The Dock for two weeks by the First Lady. "I've talked to the president, and he plans to have a word with him himself. I don't trust any fucking Lebanese. They're deceitful shit, all of them."

"Yes, sir."

Why, Stephanie wondered, as she always did, could the Lebanese possibly prefer the noise and clamor of the Denver family to his being endlessly feted in London, Paris, or New York? Could he conceivably have a crush on the first lady? Or, more likely, vice versa? He was forever seen with her and Cheryl. Was Belknap aware of it? Possibly, Stephanie had sometimes thought. Or perhaps it meant a threesome, Mara had once joked.

Tough on Belknap, whatever Cheryl was up to, Stephanie thought. She personally couldn't stand Benji, and privately called him "creep," with his forever ogling teenage grandchildren frolicking in bikinis and even in thongs in the swimming pool. Back home, women until very recently still had to wear hijabs. And in other Arab countries were even executed for daring to show their faces.

Her thoughts were jarred back to reality by her boss. "What about Sanctford?"

Secretary of State Sanctford was highly criticized by the American left for his fostering close relationships in U.S.-Saudi armament treaties. He was a man already almost elderly, and Stephanie often wondered why he'd been chosen, and how he managed to cope with the endless rigors of the job. "I believe he's well on his way, sir," she said reassuringly, "and should be here on time. He's coming along on the chopper with the Saudi representative, direct from Boston where they met."

"Warn the first lady and ask Cheryl to include him in tonight's dinner plans, if there's going to be a dinner. If the Saudis come to an agreement, then Prince What's-his-name may accept an invitation to stay over. The housekeeper should also be warned of that possibility."

"Yes, sir."

Stephanie settled at her own desk and began a string of necessary phone calls, leaving Belknap muttering to himself. She would not be party herself to the meeting called in face of mounting public pressure demanding more positive action be taken with the Saudis over their detention of the two backpacking scientists.

It was all so important and so hush-hush she almost wished she didn't know of it. Perhaps she only did because those officials surrounding the president had got so used to her and her usefulness to them that she was simply regarded as a very undangerous item, like a desk or a computer monitor. Hardly flattering, she often thought. But knowing all, although often troubling, helped her to do her job and make whatever she did more meaningful.

Five

Adrienne Denver, America's first lady, who had recently celebrated her fifty-fifth birthday, was annoyed, and the expression on her face showed it as she carefully applied makeup for the day. Her thoughts in highly private moments, when very much alone with herself, were what they always were on first arising: she hated her job.

"Damn," she muttered, leaning close to the mirror on her dressing table. "I've gone too heavy on the eye shadow." As she slowly removed some of it, she braced herself mentally for the day ahead, the endless meaningless act she'd have to perform because of the sudden diplomatic meeting with the Saudi delegation that was unexpectedly coming that afternoon, along with the secretary of state, to take over the whole day. Any plan she had of settling somewhere like the library with her iPad was ruined; or setting up her telescope on the lawn to look into the faraway universe of stars that night, the only escape she ever had from the endless misery of Washington politics.

"For Christ sake," she said again, aloud. "I'm on holiday. Or was." And began to carefully apply mascara to her eyelashes, and then, when finished, sat back to study her famous facial features, her high cheekbones, exotic dark brown eyes, and full lips. She was still strikingly beautiful, she thought.

Something in her as she did reminded her she had to speak to Aaron as soon as she was dressed. Imagining him getting dressed himself, she remembered how different he'd seemed way back when she'd first got seriously involved with him. There'd been that particular day when he'd rushed from the bed they'd shared in the Washington hotel to one of his hedge fund meetings that promised to add millions to his already considerable wealth. She all too often remembered how off-putting masculine he'd looked that early morning, his tousled hair, where now he had so little, his unshaven face, which she knew she'd soon see permanently.

How unsatisfying her nights with him, especially now, compared to those ones she'd once spent with Cheryl, and which only in a very rare while, she was still able to have.

That she'd chosen a life from which there was no escape was often more than Adrienne could bear. The success she'd had as a fashion model, with photos on the cover of *Vogue* magazine, had promised its rewards, in later careers in fashion, or perhaps even in films. Instead she'd got herself into a marriage from which there seemed no easy escape.

It was one too that had reduced herself and Cheryl to occasionally holding hands and meeting together as often as they dared, although in a way, Cheryl's marriage to Robert Belknap, her husband's Deputy Chief of Staff, who she thought was a bloated political fool, was a blessing in allowing them to be together as much as it did.

Adrienne and Cheryl had been best and intimate friends since school together at Hamilton, the elitist girl's school in Litchfield, Connecticut, where they had never tried to disguise the heavy crush they had on each other. At summer camp they'd often sneaked into the same bed, where they'd surrendered to the passion they felt for each other. Even though separated by life and each marrying to ensure financial security as well as social position, their love had in no way died, and had somehow even been strengthened by their husbands' politics.

So, never mind, Adrienne thought, bracing herself to somehow cope with yet another day married to the president, and today with a lot of special secret-meeting nonsense with some Arab and that utterly boring Secretary of State.

Her thoughts were interrupted by the sudden appearance of her daughter Beth, who, judging from her sweaty flushed appearance, her shorts, sneakers, and polo shirt, had been playing tennis.

She was proved right when Beth collapsed in a chair and said, "Guess what, Mom. I won again. And she's a good player."

Without looking, Adrienne carefully retouched one tiny area of mascara and said, "I wish you'd find something other than tennis to do all the time. Who did you play with?"

"Stephanie Crist. She played with that great team at U Penn." And then, "I see you've brought your telescope." Beth had spotted the expensive amateur telescope leaning against the wall next to her mother's dressing table. "Good idea, Mom. Air's much clearer here than in Washington. Maybe you should set it up at the top of the lighthouse. That might be even better. Nobody to bother you."

Like everyone in the family, Beth and her husband both spoke condescendingly about her mother's staring at far off stars when she couldn't name or identify a single one of them. One of her brothers said it was because their mother found an imagined someone somewhere in the firmament as more approving of her than anybody. Another brother thought it was a way to keep remembering life she'd been such a part of in the *Vogue* and *Vanity Fair* world of fashion.

"Stephanie?" Adrienne, ignoring any talk about her "scope," as she called it, drew a blank at the name, unconsciously avoiding, until forced, knowledge of anyone in her husband's administration.

"She works with Robert Belknap."

Adrienne slowly put away her mascara brush. "With Belknap?" The first lady almost spat out the name of the deputy chief of staff, whom she hated. "That little girl? But she's just an intern."

"So what? One has to start somewhere, Mom."

Adrienne wasn't having it. She turned from regarding her daughter over her shoulder in the mirror of her dressing table and said, in a coldly level voice, down-talking to her daughter as though Beth were still a child, not a married woman and a mother like herself, "Beth, for the hundredth time, please get something straight. I'll not having you demean yourself and thus me by socializing with your inferiors. Period. That young woman is no better than one of our servants."

"Oh, Mom, come on …"

"Beth! End of discussion."

Adrienne's tone was hard and unloving, and Beth, married or no, knew when not to argue. Her mother's intransigence and snobbish elitism was sometimes more than she could handle. She rose silently and left the room, leaving her mother alone with her annoyance.

With no further audience, it didn't take Adrienne long to recover. Knowing that she had to plan a reception after the Saudi meeting and with few of her usual Washington staff with her, she mentally began to do so. She'd have to notify the housekeeper immediately and land the job in her capable hands; the woman who had been brought from Washington and trained in this sort of boring thing, and while shorthanded, would have to cope. Then, if dinner, there was seating to be arranged. She'd have to put Belknap next to who, the dreary man? Surely not his wife, who was no happier with her husband than she was with being wife to the president.

Perhaps Benji, whose jet-set world appealed far more to Adrienne than what she had come to see in comparison as the shallow whirl of Washington.

Never daunted in her preference, Adrienne had assured herself of eventual post-presidency prominence in Benji's social orbit by making him often a visitor to the White House, and now had enticed him to The Dock during the White House summer month. Oxford-educated and with a nearly five-hundred-foot yacht apparently costing somewhere in the mid-nine-figures, Benji also owned a palatial estate in Barbados, a duplex penthouse in New York, and an equivalent on the Île de la Cité in Paris.

"Madam?" The sudden sound of her personal maid caused Adrienne to turn. Beatrice was standing by the room's large sofa, over which she had laid two expensive designer dresses. "I heard there is to be some sort of a reception this afternoon, madam, and thought you might want to choose now what you will wear."

Both dresses had been designed uniquely for Adrienne's five-ten frame by Claude de Versailles, one as beautiful as the other. A hard choice.

Adrienne forgot her growing jealousy over Cheryl's attachment to Benji and her annoyance with her daughter, and rose from her dressing table to choose.

<h1 style="text-align:center">Six</h1>

Leaving the office several hours later, and with Belknap off seeing the President, Stephanie located the first lady and Cheryl Belknap as well as the housekeeper. She passed on Belknap's strict order of complete secrecy about the meeting, then went quickly to a back stair that led to servants' quarters in the attic and to the room she shared with Mara.

The room was small and had been furnished with two single beds, two dressers, the minimum of closet space, and a mirror. Freed from work, Stephanie shed her tennis clothes, showered, put on jeans and a blouse, checked her makeup, which she usually kept to a minimum, then blow-dried her short chin-length blond hair.

It was her first year as one of the White House

skeletal summer staff, and she had only been at The Dock a week. The abruptly called Saudi meeting would be limited to high-level officials, which would include her boss but not her. Belknap was already tied up with it, and Stephanie with all her own preparatory work on the meeting done, virtually had the afternoon off.

Stephanie had no interest in gawking with the whole Denver family and household at the helicopter arrival of the Saudi prince and others.

Without realizing it, she had become completely blasé about important government functions, most of which she found incredibly boring and empty of any real meaning, and designed, basically, she thought, as flattery either to the visitor or to the host, depending on how you looked at it.

So, free and hardly wanting to sit around all afternoon in either the bedroom or the office, Stephanie planned to sneak off and have a look at Shinnecock and its famous lighthouse.

A well-guarded blacktop road lead to The Dock from the interstate highway some miles away. There was another and quite different way from The Dock to the village of Shinnecock. Once through a high arborvitae hedge flanking a gate at the end of the lawn, there was a narrow dirt path that ran close to the rocky shoreline and straight as an arrow to the village through a low growth of wild blueberries and milkweed with here and there scattered patches of angelica amidst banks of early goldenrod.

It was a quiet day. Not far off shore, the Coast

Guard patrol boat guarding the president lolled on a relatively calm ocean surface, it's occasional small wake when under power rocking *The Swallow,* the president's gaff-rigged sloop which he liked to sail, often on his own, and which was anchored close to the pier at the end of the lawn. Only a low lying line of cumulus clouds on the far horizon, which promised an evening shower, marred the otherwise clear sky.

Stephanie, after coming through the gate and leaving The Dock soon after lunch, felt in sheer heaven. She took her time, thinking how lucky the Denver grandchildren were to be at The Dock, and loving the short walk until, nearly at the end of the path, reality checked in.

Directly in front of her, any entrance to Shinnecock was blocked by one of a score of state troopers now in Shinnecock, along with an SUV and a Secret Service agent, both holding back a dozen paparazzi as well as a small crowd of tourists. The trooper's distinctive uniform and hat, the agent's suit, his dark glasses, the SUV all broadcast no-nonsense state and federal authority, and Stephanie had hardly taken in their presence when she felt laughter lurking inside her. She suffered no qualms at seeing them. Secret Service personnel to her were only a tedious necessity, many serving as just uniformed cops who might as well have been directing traffic as well as making a show of guarding the president.

Stephanie Crist was not a young woman who

was cowed by authority which she herself if not unnecessarily pushed, respectfully recognized as necessary. She could claim none of the background so many driven successful young women did. She had not had an abusive father, her parents were not divorced or lived in poverty, she had never had to overcome a disability or physical disadvantage.

Quite the contrary. Stephanie's father was a respected neurosurgeon at prestigious Mass General, her mother a senior public health authority. Both her brothers had gone to Yale and one was already a successful lawyer. She had a life full of privilege and got a job interning at the White House largely through pull by her mother's close relationship with the health advisor to the president. Honoring her luck, as she always put it even to herself, and even to her own surprise, she had ended up an intern and personal assistant to the powerful deputy chief of staff, a job that brought with it a closeness to the president himself along with most of his renowned family.

Her position, however, did not in any way make her think herself better than others less fortunate. Stephanie was a modest person who recognized how lucky the roulette of life had been that had brought her into being with a loving family along with opportunities that many her age missed out on.

The trooper and the Secret Service agent put aside paper coffee cups as Stephanie approached, and in the two years she had been working at the

White House, Stephanie had learned the form. Play respectful and show ID. She did both, pulling the small card with her picture and name out from the protective cover of her blouse and cardigan.

"Good morning," she said. "I'm aide to Mr. Belknap."

The Secret Service agent took a long and pointed look at the ID before saying "Yes, ma'am," and handing it back. Stephanie thanked him and walked around the SUV and pushed through the tourists. *Job really does have its perks,* she thought.

Seven

There wasn't much to Shinnecock, Stephanie found, that she hadn't already imagined. It was a well-kept New England small town with clapboarded or shingled exteriors on most of the houses, and she felt friendly to it almost at once. A few dozen houses fanned out each side of those that lined its macadam main street, identifiable in its short length by stores typical to any main street anywhere in America and reaping the rewards brought to Shinnecock after a long slow winter by the many tourists ogling and buying everything they normally would not have.

Stephanie had to wonder what Shinnecock had to look like when snow melted from rooftops and was pushed up against the curb or shoveled away from store fronts. *Like everyplace else,* she thought, and *just not so hot.*

She still had time and decided on the lighthouse. She'd already heard it talked about one day by Cheryl Belknap, along with the First Lady, both speaking at once and seemingly anxious to show off ownership through the Denver Trust. There again, her way was blocked by another small mob of tourists held back by the Secret Service guarding any entrance to the path from the bottom of Main Street and the shore to the narrow rocky neck which led to the lighthouse.

Stephanie got past them, and then when on the narrow neck itself, and thinking how any serious storm would wash right over it, completely isolating the lighthouse, saw the trim figure of a young woman in jeans at the base of the lighthouse itself. She was standing at the door of a small stone house which had a round iron chimney protruding from its shingled roof and was attached to the base of the lighthouse, and she appeared to be talking to a rough-appearing older man who wore rubber boots and worn work clothes that looked as though he'd slept in them.

Stephanie didn't have to wait long to find out who they were. The woman in turn spotted her, and instantly leaving the little stone house, came up the causeway to her, letting Stephanie see more clearly that although in jeans, she wore a police badge pinned to an ordinary work shirt, and had around her waist a police officer's utility belt with a low-slung holstered Glock, a phone, a taser, and cuffs.

"You're who?" she demanded of Stephanie. Her voice sounded no-nonsense.

"Stephanie Crist," Stephanie replied, and once again flashed her ID card. "My first summer here. I'm working down at The Dock."

Clearly unimpressed, Angi took a small black notebook from a hip pocket and compared a list of names in it to the name on Stephanie's ID card. "Crist, you said? You know that this is private property?" She eyed Stephanie carefully, and deciding, a little surprised, that Stephanie didn't seem one of the usual White House snobs who came every summer, she then smiled and said, "Okay, I guess."

Okay? It left Stephanie with a mild sense of indignation. The Denver family owned the lighthouse, didn't they? What was a town cop doing judging who could look at it and who couldn't? But before she could protest she heard the police officer say, as though reading her mind and with less of the police officer in her voice, "I'm the town cop from the force at Barthchester. Family's request. Keep an eye on the lighthouse for them." She laughed. "Make sure the Secret Service and state police goons or anybody else don't steal anything." And then, looking Stephanie up and down, "Out looking around, are you?"

Friendly enough for me, Stephanie thought. *I'll certainly go along with it.* She smiled and said, "I intern with the deputy chief of staff. Got a work break this afternoon."

Angi said, "Angi Cajun. Welcome to Shinnecock," and without realizing it, did something she never did, and stuck out her hand.

Stephanie responded, and they shook, and Angi said, "Show you around, if you'd like," and Stephanie eyeing the towering lighthouse, said, "Sure. Does it still work?"

"Hardly. Gave up the ghost years back to GPS or some fancy electronic nonsense."

The man she'd been talking to ignored Stephanie's appearance and began dragging a lobster trap, along with its painted buoy, from several stacked by the little stone house, down steps to the water, where a small open boat was moored to an iron ring sunk into one of the massive rocks holding up the lighthouse. Lobster traps, big square slat-sided boxes, were stacked on its long open deck aft of a wheel cabin in its bow.

Seeing Stephanie's curiosity, Angi laughed. "Just Farney," she said. "Farney Gould. Been here for years. His old man before him. The family, sometime way back, allowed them to lobster here. Come to Farney, he wasn't going to budge either until he had a bona fide court order saying so."

Stephanie watched the rough old lobsterman a moment longer as he dumped the lobster trap onto the deck of the put-put lobster boat, and got onto the boat himself, and started its motor. When it pulled away, she followed Angi to the door of the towering lighthouse which Angi unlocked with a large old-fashioned key she took from behind a small hinged bronze plaque with SHINNECOCK

LIGHTHOUSE written on it, along with 1798.

"I try to remember to keep it locked most of the time," she said, "Although it's like, what's the point, since anyone could find this old key."

She used it to first unlock then swing open the heavy stone door on rusty iron hinges, and Stephanie found herself in near darkness and in a relatively enclosed space dominated by a narrow, tightly spiraling and steep iron stair with no rail, and where a user was supported only by the lighthouse's outside wall. Her heart sank. She was terrified of heights, and this?

"Have to make a bit of a climb," she heard the young police officer say. And then, "No rail, so hug the wall."

Without further word she nimbly started up the iron steps, leaning against the wall as she went.

Oh, my God, what have I got myself into, Stephanie thought, and her heart in her mouth, she started up the stair after her. Being a good athlete didn't mean she had any head for heights. From childhood, she'd been plagued by frightening vertigo.

Eight

Heart in her mouth, trying not to think or even be aware, Stephanie, step-by-step, and angrily refusing to surrender to ever increasing misery, followed Angi upward in near darkness, with the only light coming through an open trap door high above.

Once, looking down into the yawning dark below her, she almost gave up, but was forced to continue by the seemingly nonchalant and unaffected figure of the town cop climbing steadily upward, sometimes a few steps in front of her and sometimes alongside, but never hesitating except to pause to emphasize a word as she talked.

"This is a weekly and summertime daily climb for me," Angi said. And next, "Or maybe more, if I think someone has beat me to it, and what do you know but often someone has gone and done just that. Trust me. I've had my share of catching teens making out up here, not to mention their being stripped naked and going at it like they'd never get another chance."

She laughed. "Or drunks. Will never know how one guy made it and didn't fall five stories. So pissed he couldn't stand. He didn't have a bottle on him when I got to him, meaning he was already pretty much gone when he started up. Belligerent idiot. I cuffed him to the lighting machinery and left him there until I thought he could make it back down without dragging me with him."

Several times, Stephanie felt the young officer's hands on her, holding her fast against the lighthouse wall to keep her from slipping off the railless iron stair, but finally, and weak with relief, she reached the open trapdoor at the top and was able to half crawl through it on her own onto the floor of a small circular room surrounded by heavy glass windows.

For a moment she closed her eyes against the sudden light, then getting to her feet, she saw, half filling the center of the room and on top of a massive group of heavy clockwork-like gears, a large turntable that looked like a big flat wheel surrounding a solid hub that stood in its the middle.

"There's your light, or what used to be the light," Angi offered. She pointed to two big curved mirrors on top of the turntable.

"Those two mirrors, they're actually complicated

lenses. As the turntable slowly revolves around and around, they reflect the lantern's light at intervals."

"But what makes the turntable turn?" Stephanie asked. She had begun to recover from the climb.

"That three-hundred-pound weight there," Angi explained. "Takes just two hours for it to unwind from the big drum and slowly drop all the way to the bottom of the lighthouse. Then it has to be cranked back up. Meant that the lightkeeper had to climb up here four times every night to keep the lights flashing regular. I don't know, but maybe he slept up here. I sure as hell would have."

"Does it still work?" Stephanie asked.

"Only more or less," Angi said. She pressed down a projecting lever, and the turntable began to turn. She lifted the lever back up, the turntable stopped, and with difficulty she turned a hand crank. The big gears groaned and began to move. She stopped cranking and said, "Have to mind the gears. Couldn't crank the weight back up without them, but they could catch clothing. I gave them a drop of oil and ran it all the way once just to see, but don't dare do that again. It's so old it's plain worn out, poor thing."

She broke off with a laugh. "Got all that? Sorry. I must sound like a tour guide."

"No, you don't. It's fascinating," Stephanie said. She was completely surprised by all the young policewoman knew. "You know so much."

"My job to," Angi said.

"Well, I'm really impressed. Do they still run

actual tours up here?"

"They used to, before my time, but not any-more. Not since Aaron Denver became the current president. Secret Service won't allow it. president's a clean sniper shot from up here."

Stephanie said, "I think I heard Adrienne Denver was planning to bring up her telescope. She spends hours when not doing her first lady job, staring at the stars, although nobody knows why. She doesn't know one star from another. Just looks out into infinity. Escape, I guess."

"Jesus Christ," Angi said. "The first lady? She's coming up here. Waste of time, you ought to tell her. Windows so damned dirty what with grime from salt spray and all, you could hardly see any stars through them."

"Can't they be washed?" Stephanie offered.

"Possibly," Angi said. "But not by me. No way. Rickety old iron platform that wraps around the outside is half rusted away. Got to be nuts to even think of standing on it, let alone wash windows."

A certain loyalty that was simply part of her nature, even if she didn't particularly feel it where the first lady was concerned, stopped Stephanie from further words where the telescope was con-cerned. Keeping curiosity to oneself, or suppressing it entirely, and as much as possible, she routinely avoided thoughts or any talk on the first lady's per-sonal life. Adrienne Denver's endless conflict with the Secret Service was notorious among the inner staff of the White House. She was often imperiously at odds with them, giving them the slip whenever she could, or ending up in an angry confrontation. White House employees, Stephanie and her friend Mara Harmon among them, were forever finding themselves unwilling witnesses to outbursts of uncontrolled anger.

"Seen enough?" She heard Angi say. "Let's go, then. I've probably got problems down below to take care of." She laughed. "Cop's day is never done."

Stephanie took a deep breath. She knew going down would be perhaps even more difficult than coming up. Steeling herself, she followed Angi through the trapdoor and onto the perilous staircase.

"Stay close to the wall," Angi said.

"Don't worry," Stephanie said. She had never in her life before felt so dependent on another person or such unexpected closeness.

Nine

For Stephanie, going back down the narrow spiraling iron stair was even worse than she had imagined. Her entire body weak with fear, she pressed herself against the wall of the lighthouse, and with every step tried not to think about the dark void below. When finally reaching the bottom, she could barely find either words or even breath to respond to Angi's cheerful comment, "Not so bad then, was it?"

"Not for you, maybe." Stephanie managed a weak smile and added, "But bless you for the tour. It was spectacular."

Angi laughed. "In more ways than one, I guess. Sorry for the stair."

Stephanie managed good humor back. "Need an assistant helping people up and down, just ask." She still couldn't quite believe how pleasantly understanding this cop was. She felt she'd known her forever. A glance at her watch told her that alarmingly, she'd stayed far longer than she'd planned. Belknap might be looking for her.

"My pleasure. Any time," Angi said when they parted ways, and Stephanie, after thanking her once more, then slipped past the paparazzi and the Secret Service detail to the path through the gorse and blueberries and angelica wildflowers lining the way to the arborvitae hedge and the gate to the lawn surrounding The Dock.

Angi, watching her, was sorry to see her go. She'd liked being with her even though briefly and although one of the Summer White House bunch. *Nice person,* she thought. And at the same time felt a pang of envy. Oh, to live in a house like The Dock. Out of sheer curiosity, she had visited it several times on long winter months when the swimming pool was covered, and a blanket of snow was on the lawns, and with the storm shutters of the big house closed on most of the windows. *A big kitchen and all the hot water anyone could wish for,* she thought. *And my own bedroom too.*

Her much different home had always been her parents' one-bedroom row house, her father working for the Boston Sanitation Department heaving the contents of garbage cans into the back of a big truck, her mother washing dishes in the kitchen of a fast-food diner. Both had always hoped to send Angi to college, but together they had never made enough money, and Angi had been obliged to settle for high school, taking a bus there every morning in a twenty-five-minute ride. The government had paid for police academy, with neighbors chipping in to help.

On her part, and walking the narrow path from Shinnecock back to The Dock, Stephanie felt a glow of pleasure at her visit and a sudden sense of famil-iarity with the old lighthouse as well as remember-ing a sense of comradeship with the young police officer who had helped her up the stair. *Not at all like most cops,* she thought.

Her thinking about her adventuresome trip up to the top of the lighthouse stopped, however, the moment she reached the gate in the arborvitae hedge barring the way to the Denver family home and was then struck by something unusual. It was silence.

Not a shout nor the shrill cries of Denver grandchildren at water polo disturbed it. It was so quiet Stephanie could hear water lapping the rocks on the shore. And she had hardly registered this fact, and then that full secrecy with all the grand-children was in effect because of the scheduled meeting with the Saudis, when she heard first the distant whisper then, louder and louder, the heavy *blatt-blatt* of the approaching helicopter blades as the giant bird slowly descended onto the landing pad on the lawn beyond the tennis courts.

Back in the office of the deputy chief of staff, she found Belknap already gone to join the president in greeting Secretary of State Bruce Sanctford and the accompanying royal Saudi emissary, Prince Ahmed Faisal bin Tala, son of the Saudi ruler Mohammed bin Salaman. The prince and his foreign minister wearing their traditional kaffiyeh with its circling *iqal* seemed oddly out of place.

Held well back with other lesser important staff by Secret Service personnel who had appeared as though from nowhere to form a virtual cordon protecting the arrivals and their welcomers, Stephanie briefly wondered why she had ever bothered returning from her escape to Shinnecock and its famous lighthouse.

Watching the arriving party, the president, her boss, and the secretary of state along with the Saudi Arabs, all indulging in a ritual of hand shaking as the president welcomed the prince, she mentally scheduled the rest of the president's day and thus Belknap's. She knew Belknap would be kept close at hand by the president, with Hank Whittaker, his own immediate boss and the all-powerful chief of staff back in Washington, attending the meeting by video.

The meeting itself would be held in the book-lined library of the big summer house and was bound to last several hours. Unlike herself, Mara Harmon would be invited to it to maintain a journalistic report for the Washington press office. Dolly Bridges and Aura Sin, deputy assistants to the national security adviser and the national director of intelligence, respectively, had come with the secretary of state from Washington and had met the visiting emissaries at Boston for the helicopter flight to The Dock.

Then, after the meeting, there'd be an informal reception in which everyone would act as though there'd been success in getting the hostages freed, whether or not there had been. The whole Denver family would be in attendance, except for the grandchildren, who once again would be held at bay by their three nannies.

Reaching her desk, Stephanie imagined it all and was wondering how she would dress for the reception—she'd brought the barest minimum in the way of clothes, but perhaps she could borrow from Mara—when she was jarred out of her thoughts by a voice almost in her ear. "I hope I have the honor of sharing champagne with you at the reception after all the big names solve world problems."

Turning quickly, and to her dismay, she found herself looking up at Benji, the first lady's famous guest.

Stephanie steeled herself. The Lebanese billionaire playboy's handsome heavily tanned face, with its close cropped beard and mustache, was uncomfortably close. She instinctively drew back and held her breath against the strong odor of his expensive men's talc and eau de cologne. Caught completely off guard and at a loss for words, she managed a smile to hide her thorough dislike of the man, and at the same time pushed her chair away slightly.

"Been looking around for you all morning," she heard him say. "Where have you been?" The smile that accompanied the question was one Stephanie recognized, as any young woman instantly would, as his coming on to her.

This wasn't the first uncomfortable moment for her with the Lebanese. Although famous and with movie star good looks, his persistent appearance when she was alone had ruined much of her off-duty time at The Dock, especially since she had inadvertently learned that Benji, although generally presumed and accepted as thoroughly clean by his peers, the public, and especially by the Justice Department's FBI, had something of a shady past.

It was rumored among some that he had been or even was an illegal arms dealer, that he had high-level contact with a Russian oligarch believed a front and financier for many of the aggressive foreign activities of the Kremlin, and that he had amassed his not inconsiderable fortune through endless other illicit dealings.

Stephanie found herself believing all of it, if nobody else did, and it was a mystery to her why the president's wife had such a clearly warm friendship with the man, or worse, why the president himself continued to find him acceptable.

She was still struggling to find a response when she was rescued by Cheryl, who appeared magically in the office arm in arm with none other than the first lady herself. Both women were expensively casual. Stephanie hardly had time to wonder at the first lady's presence, certain she'd never been in the special office wing of The Dock before, when Adrienne Denver said, "Benji, stop your flirting and come with us." It was a command, to which she added with a condescending smile in Stephanie's direction. "The girl has work to do, I'm sure."

Benji didn't need to be told twice, and to Stephanie's relief, she saw the jet-set Lebanese being escorted out of the office and back toward the main wing of the house. She supposed coping with unwanted flirting was part of her job, in fact any job anywhere. Just the same, she found the visitor celebrity especially unwanted. She wondered what her boss's wife found in him so interesting. Cheryl could hardly be accused, in Stephanie's mind, of looking around for kicks with any man other than her husband. She had too much going socially by being attached to him. Attached, yes, except for an equal seeming attachment to the first lady.

Cheryl and Adrienne. Both, when immersed in the Washington political scene, appeared to have remained as bonded now, Stephanie thought, as they reputedly had been in school where, for many, crushes were par for the course. They were forever together, sometimes almost intimately close, as right now when she observed them with their arms around each other's waists as they left with Benji.

With a mild shock, she also realized that she had never seen either Cheryl or Adrienne exhibit the same closeness with either of their husbands. It was as though they were still at school with each other. Had they never grown up?

Ten

Charles Sanctford was a graying, nearly skeletal man with a quavering voice and hands that shook when he ate hors d'oeuvres and sipped champagne at the reception for the Saudis after the secret meeting was over. Along with the Saudi prince and Saudi foreign minister, he pretended the secret meeting a success where the two American scientists the kingdom held hostage were concerned when in fact it had resolved nothing. The Saudis, Mara said to Stephanie when they found a moment together, had not yielded an inch, while hiding with relaxed smiles and affability their unyielding position that both hostages had been caught engaged in espionage.

"Geopolitical nonsense," Mara said, and Stephanie agreed. She'd felt a complete outsider to the conference during the afternoon and knew Mara felt the same, even though as Summer White House press secretary she'd actually been involved.

The first lady had reverted to the formal manner she always wore on official occasions when accompanying her husband or when on her own, performing her numerous civic duties. Being first lady was a personality which she removed like a mask when she was at home with family. But during the afternoon reception, and in spite of her temporarily assumed formality, her chatting with Benji reminded Stephanie that his celebrity status and personal wealth had always impressed the first lady as far preferable to her own. As a silent observer, she found it hard to understand the first lady's attachment to the Lebanese, to whom she seemed as close as she was to Belknap's wife.

Of more immediate importance to Stephanie was the behavior of her boss. Belknap's drinking too much, as he put on a show of pretending hospitality he didn't feel, made her uncomfortable and once actually alarmed at what she saw as overly loose and talkative bonhomie when talking about U.S. military strategy with the Saudi foreign minister. She had summoned up courage, and catching his attention, nodded at his champagne glass and said, "Sir?" with a smile, then shaking her head slightly, hoping others wouldn't notice, moved away quickly, also hoping he wouldn't remember her warning.

Relieved when the reception was over, Stephanie retired first to the office to write a quick log of the day's events, then to the attic room she shared with Mara where, after immediately erasing as fast as possible any thoughts of the useless meeting to free the hostages, she wondered why she was working at all in Washington. The failed meeting that afternoon had made her realize that she couldn't go more upward than she already had. She had no bent for politics or any political office. She would be stuck in the White House where she was an intern until the administrations changed, and then what? A sort of oblivion unless hired for a minor position by one of the broadcast networks, or perhaps one of Washington's think tanks or some lobbyist organization. It had all seemed so exciting at first, and now it was all so terribly stale.

Dismally, she realized she hadn't yet met any guy coming onto her, among the scores who had, whom she'd considered for a lifetime affair: for sharing life first with him, whomever he would be, then with children. The thought further depressed her as later she got ready for bed with Mara already ahead of her and asleep, all her journalistic instincts frustrated on the strict silence imposed on the press division.

When Stephanie finally pulled up the covers herself, overwhelmingly exhausted, it was to try to resist reviewing all of the day all over again. She found herself thinking again of the young cop she'd gone up to the top of the lighthouse with. What was her name? Angi? Her first sort-of typical police hostility, then the friendliness and later the kindness in her voice when descending, the cop had protectively pressed her against the wall while precariously close to the edge of the spiral stair herself. And the cop saying, "Hang in there, gal, we're more than halfway."

Stephanie found herself wondering why she was a police officer. She didn't seem like one at all. And how had she become one in the first place? She wondered where the woman lived, what her family was like. Did she have brothers and sisters, or was she an only child, and who were her parents? Obviously decent people. How different she was, Stephanie thought, from all those she worked with, save for Mara: the sort of down-to-earth honesty about her in her straightforward bluntness that was so missing among the Belknaps of the world.

And then, in the last few moments before she fell asleep, Stephanie found herself briefly wondering about Belknap's troubling loose talk at the reception. It didn't match up with the strange kind of secrecy he often displayed when huddled over his laptop at his desk and that she had often seen back in Washington. She found it disturbing. Was there something in Belknap's life that he was hiding, or was it just his anxiety when he was sober over remembering his loose talk when drinking?

Whatever it was, it kept Stephanie worrying that if Belknap had some serious problem, it could reflect on her and cost her job as well as be dangerous where security was concerned.

Eleven

A week later, life at The Dock had returned to relative normalcy. The Saudi prince and the secretary of state were long gone, the helicopter swooping low over Shinnecock before rising nearly out of sight and banking away to the north and Boston, where the prince's plane waited to return him to Saudi Arabia. Their departure was celebrated by a quick return of the endless shouts and cries of Denver grandchildren playing water polo in the swimming pool. "We're supposed to be running a country, not a nursery," was the oft repeated sour comment of one of the audiovisual technicians.

The return to work saw the two interns, Mara, and Stephanie with nothing else to do evenings after days of grueling hard work but compare gossip and notes on their current jobs, as well as past ones, and talking about college years, Stephanie's rise up the tennis tournament ladder, and Mara being totally unathletic.

"In fifty tries, I never once sank a basketball through the hoop," Mara said, laughing. And then, more soberly, "To say nothing of coping with anti-Semitism. It makes you both fearful of some people and angry at them at the same time. What's the matter with the world?"

When there was a letup in work for a while, and both interns took a much needed break, Stephanie decided to show Mara Shinnecock and its famous historic lighthouse.

"Not a problem for me," she said. "I need things at the pharmacy for a start. And there's a good pizza place if we can fight our way through the tourists to get to it."

With Mara not objecting, they set off right after lunch, at the same time that the town cop was bemoaning the horde of tourists. They had kept Angi busy since the day began, filling the main street like a tsunami. And there'd been all the usual nuisances when it came to the lighthouse. There'd been a drunk she'd had to handcuff and turn over to a state trooper, the usual vandals, this time two tiresome teenage girls whom she'd had to get especially tough with, then an ugly argument with one of the Secret Service detail who constantly appeared, wherever she was, to ask what she was doing. It did no good to request help from her chief down at Barchester, just as it did to ask for help from the several state troopers. "Busy with the president," was their constant refusal. She was on her own.

A close-by voice interrupted Angi's momentary annoyance. Leaning against one of the Secret Service's black SUVs, she was brought back to reality from imagining the end of the day and, if she were lucky, her evening two-mile run, and then a shower and bed.

"Hi, Angi. Remember me?" And Angi found herself looking at the woman she'd escorted to the top of the lighthouse some days ago. What was her name? And another woman with her whom she didn't recognize.

"Stephanie Crist," Stephanie said, seeing Angi draw a blank.

It all came back to Angi in a rush: helping the woman cope with the narrow spiral iron stair. The scary trip back down, when for a moment she was fearful that the panic she knew the woman was in might be the end of them both. And yes, talking about the first lady stargazing.

"Oh, hi," she said. "Caught me far away someplace. Back for more?"

"Not me," Stephanie replied. "But my friend is dying to see the lighthouse. We could go it alone if you're too busy."

She introduced Mara, who Angi stared at a moment before demanding her ID, and even as Mara, a little surprised, obeyed, fished out her notebook from a hip pocket, realizing at the same time that doing so was probably ridiculous. "Sorry," she said. "Got to recognize formalities. Never can tell."

Stephanie took a pass on going back up the iron stair that wound its perilous way to the top of the old lighthouse. "Once was enough, thank you," she said, and to Mara, "Good luck, and cover your head," provoking a laugh when Mara, who although with no fear of heights or danger, worried if she might encounter bats in the darkness.

When both Angi and she had disappeared into the base of the towering lighthouse, Stephanie settled down to wait, finding a seat on a large rock, and from time to time having a word with Farney Gould, who would appear from within the little stone cottage lugging empty and dried-out traps to stack them on the open flat deck of his little lobster boat.

"Do you go out every day?" she asked.

"Yup. From before sunup," he told her. "Then down to the commercial docks."

"But what do you do when the weather's real bad?"

"Go anyway," the lobsterman grunted. "Got to earn a living."

Come hell or high water, I guess, Stephanie thought, thinking of often miserable mornings with Belknap when the deputy chief of staff had a hangover. *Like all the rest of us.*

When eventually Mara and Angi reappeared, it was with a burst of outright delight from Mara. "Wow! Stephanie, what a view."

Angi in turn said, and in a different tone, "Something up there that wasn't there your trip. A fancy telescope lying on the floor. Maybe a couple of days by the look of it since it's never been set up. Do I remember right your saying you'd heard the first lady might bring hers up. Well, she'll have to take it the hell down again if she's not planning to use it. I can't be responsible for it being stolen. And there's no way that I can be up here twenty-four hours guarding it."

"Adrienne Denver?" Mara said in surprise when Stephanie explained about the first lady's stargazing. "How did she get it up here? Not by herself, surely." The president's wife's aversion to any sort of work was well known.

Stephanie said, "I suspect she probably paid Farney to do it." She explained who Farney was, and said, "He'd pulled his boat up to the float at the end of the pier, and I saw her talking to him when I was on my lunch hour the day after the big meeting, and she had the telescope with her."

Angi said, "Sounds right. The old devil. If he was the one who brought it up, he probably charged her a bunch for it too, I bet."

She'd hardly spoken when Farney Gould himself came out of the little stone house, dragging yet another lobster trap decorated with wisps of dried-out clinging seaweed.

"Farney," Angi said. "That telescope up top that you hauled up for Mrs. Denver?"

"Telescope?"

"Thing laying on the floor by the light. Seems she's not using it, so when you have time, bring it back down and boat it back to The Dock, okay? I don't want it up there anymore. You neither. All the people around, could get stolen and fingers pointed at me as well as you."

Farney began to disentangle the long rope attached to a brightly painted little buoy at the end that would mark the trap's location. When he spoke he sounded truculent.

"Telescope's none of your business. First lady waved me into the pier day after the damned chopper quit buzzing all over and had me bring it up here. 'You're in charge of it,' she said. 'And don't let nobody come and fool with it or bring it back down unless its me.'"

The lobsterman took an angry breath and glared at Angi. "So ain't no thief is gonna lay a hand on it, bet your life on it, and I ain't touching it myself until the first lady, God bless her, tells me to."

Clearly done talking, Farney continued dragging the trap and buoy with him to his boat, leaving a momentary silence behind him that was first broken by Stephanie, who exchanged a look with Angi and said, "I'll try to have a word with Mrs. Denver."

"Yeah," Angi said. "Good idea."

Twelve

Work again took over first thing the next morning, the way it had right after the Saudi visit: a continued forceful reminder to both interns that they were still in the Summer White House, with all the importance of the liaison between its skeletal administrative staff and the Oval Office in Washington.

For Stephanie, it was all back to normal, with Belknap more demanding than usual and clearly in a bad mood, and with Mara being harried by yet more endless questions on the secret visit of the Saudi prince that she had already answered and which would never be read.

And for both young women there was the often jarring contrast and contradiction between the seriousness of what they did and the Denver family life. The tennis court again resounded with the swat of racquet against ball, while the disrupting shrill shouts and screams of the grandchildren in the swimming pool filled nearly every corner of The Dock.

Back to normal, however, would not be for long for either Stephanie or Mara or anyone else in the Summer White House, including the president.

Nor, especially, for the Barthchester police force's young cop assigned to keep whatever law and order possible in the village of Shinnecock. It fell on Angi to break that normalcy.

On a following Sunday morning that found Stephanie again playing first-of-the-day tennis with Beth Harquist, and Mara on the shore inspecting and making notes on varieties of life she found among the rocks, Angi rose late from the upstairs room she rented each summer in a private house to rush to the village to cope with the first influx of visitors that would swell to a tsunami like wave as the day wore on.

She had hardly suited up when she had to first block the way to the lighthouse to a tour group, then to a noisy pair of middle schoolers. She was about to take a break for coffee up the street at the pizza parlor when she spotted one of the paparazzi who had managed to get onto the narrow stone causeway leading out to the lighthouse, unobserved either by the Secret Service or a trooper.

"Oh, shit," Angi muttered. "Give me a break," and briefly abandoning thoughts of coffee, she elbowed past two Secret Service men, who, seeing her pursuit, laughed and said, "Go get him, copper," with herself replying, "And fuck you too," as she pursued. She got to the paparazzo just as he had reached the lighthouse. But he wasn't after a look at the famous once guardian of the rocky shore. He was after a long range photo shot of The Dock, and had started to swing his camera in its direction when Angi collared him.

"You're off limits, mister. Back where you came from on the double, or you get cuffed and arrested."

It took a moment for the paparazzo to register that Angi was a police officer. When he did he decided his planned shot wasn't worth it, and sullenly muttering curses, he went back up the narrow causeway to Main Street.

Angi didn't follow immediately. Habits don't die easily, and almost without thinking, she tried the door to the lighthouse to make sure it was locked. It wasn't. It swung partially open, then stopped as though blocked by something. A hundred quick thoughts flashed though Angi's mind; first, why was the door unlocked, then, what could be stopping the door from opening fully.

None were clear. She pushed against the blockage and stepped into the gloom of the towering structure.

Angi had seen a lot of death as a cop. She was tough. But just the same, she saw that the door had been blocked by a body, and it took her only seconds to see who it was. When she did, she gasped in shock.

Lying very dead with his head smashed in from falling the five stories from the top of the lighthouse was the more than familiar figure of Farney Gould.

Thirteen

Angi was a good cop. She was well trained and had extensive experience with the organized Barthchester police before being assigned in the summer to enforce the law in Shinnecock as the village town cop. More importantly, she liked the job, with all its responsibilities and in spite of its drawbacks.

Just the same, her mind and any thinking for a few moments was frozen with astonishment that she was looking down not just at a dead person, lying unexpectedly, of all places, in the lighthouse, but that she was looking at Farney Gould. The inert dead body was that of someone she knew well, and the very last person who she or anyone else would likely ever find dead there.

Overcoming her first shock, she managed to

suppress personal feelings. One moment her mind was frozen, and the next she'd recovered with a maze of conflicting thoughts as she sought to find some reason for Farney having fallen, or, for that matter, why in the first place he had climbed up the stairs to the very top of the lighthouse only to fall all the way down from way up there, which he must have done to have his head so badly injured, his limbs twisted awkwardly.

She couldn't make his doing so fit. Farney had never shown any interest in the lighthouse save for the few bucks she thought he might have got by taking the telescope up to the top for the first lady. And as for falling, that wasn't Farney.

Old as he was, Farney was still a strong able man who constantly scrambled in and out of his little lobster boat with never a slip. It made Angi sure he never could have fallen all by himself. Someone had to have pushed him off the narrow spiral stair, and with that, Angi realized she was looking at a possible homicide.

She moved quickly. She unhooked her phone from her belt, and punched in the one button that instantly connected her with Barthchester police headquarters.

"Officer Cajun, up at Shinnecock. Code red. Got a death here at the lighthouse that maybe isn't accidental. I'll notify troopers and will seal off possible crime scene. Awaiting orders."

Running back up the narrow causeway, she collared a state trooper she found chatting idly with the two Secret Service officers who had jeered at her going down the causeway after the paparazzi.

"Got a problem. Base of the lighthouse. Local guy who got by you is dead. Very. I've just linked in Barthchester. They're sending a unit. Stop anybody from going down there while I get tape."

She abandoned the startled trooper and Secret Service agents, and after fetching a never used before POLICE—CRIME SCENE tape from the office, enlisted their help in stretching it across the causeway.

It was exactly 9 a.m. in what was to be a grueling day. The Barthchester homicide crime unit moved rapidly. Several uniforms and two detectives arrived within an hour, along with the Barthchester police chief, Mike Carvalho. The coroner came a half hour later, and there was a silence among all of them that would not have prevailed with the death of an unknown. Most knew Farney, even if only as a familiar figure in his little lobster boat putt-putting up and down the coast in the early mornings. He had always seemed a part of Shinnecock itself, and Barthchester too.

That his death was indeed one of homicide was quickly identified as such by the coroner, a no-nonsense middle-aged woman who wore her medical authority as an aggressive weapon and to whom death was a daily occupation. After a short examination of the corpse, during which she ignored Farney's shattered head and badly broken limbs, she announced he had not died from the fall. His death, she said, had preceded it. He'd died from a ligature strangulation. A medallion chain Farney had always worn was found deeply embedded in his neck.

The pronouncement came as a hard-to-believe additional shock to everyone, Angi among them. After a brief huddle with Mike Carvalho, in which she gave him a general picture of the lighthouse and what she knew of its intended use by the first lady, whom the deceased said he had assisted in her stargazing plan, two detectives, one named Grace Schmidt, the other Arthur Combe, climbed the treacherous spiraling upward iron stair to the light platform some five stories above the sea. It took only minutes for both detectives to come to the conclusion that Farney Gould had climbed up there for reasons yet unknown and had either interrupted or himself been interrupted in a possible attempted robbery.

The telescope had clearly been disturbed as well as removed from where Angi, who'd come up with them, said it had lain the day before. Although its smaller viewing scope was still attached, as well as the big lens at its end, the protective canvas cover for the big lens was lying loose on the floor a few feet distant.

"We'll want Forensic on this one," Combe pronounced almost at once, with Schmidt agreeing and saying, "Bound to be fingerprints on just about everything and maybe DNA."

A requested state forensic unit came within hours. It took prints and DNA from everything everywhere, from the telescope and its lens, from the steel floor and the trapdoor and the stairs, to the turntable surface above the big rotation gears where the reflecting mirrors and kerosene lamps had once flashed warning of the dangerous hidden shelf to passing mariners.

The floor was blue-lighted to reveal bloodstains, which were found to be numerous, and down below, Farney Gould's lifeless broken corpse was photographed from every possible angle before being taken away to the morgue in the coroner's wagon, which had pushed its way through a gathering curious crowd at the bottom of Main Street.

Knowing that the lighthouse was private property, not part of the Shinnecock village but belonging to the Denver family at The Dock through a trust, Mike Carvalho, already in touch with the district attorney in Barthchester for a warrant, mentally selected who would have to be informed in the Denver family. Not the president, surely. The chief quailed at the thought of disturbing him with something as mundane as a strictly local homicide while simultaneously cursing whomever had perpetrated a murder in his precinct and so under his official surveillance.

A quick discussion with Angi, checking full names from her notebook, produced both Stephanie and Mara as government employees attached to the administration and members of what people were calling the Summer White House. Both, the young town cop said, had met the deceased while visiting the lighthouse, one of them twice, and had seen the telescope left lying on the steel plate floor supporting the antique remains of the famous tower's flashing light.

But, Chief Carvalho thought, he would need to connect with somebody more important in what was a perhaps difficult political situation. A man had been murdered on property belonging to the President of the United States, and running down a list of White House summer staff, which he'd been given at the beginning of the president's residence, the chief rapidly came up with the deputy chief of staff, the person in charge of all the White House employees present, and if he remembered correctly, that meant a man named Robert Belknap.

The chief steeled himself, reminded himself that he was the law, and accompanied by the two detectives, and armed with the warrant he'd quickly received by email from the district attorney, he left the lighthouse to make his way through the tourists and paparazzi onto the path that led to The Dock.

Fourteen

S ome news travels slowly, even news of a homicide, and it was some time before anybody at The Dock, including Stephanie, heard of what had happened to Farney Gould. The first person to be confronted by the chief and his two detectives was, of all people, one of the nannies who was on the porch where French glass doors led to the living room. She was shepherding a group of small children into the house.

Startled at the unexpected appearance of police, she could barely reply to Chief Carvalho's heavily authoritative question as to where he could find Robert Belknap. But when she had collected herself long enough to, she said she thought Mr. Belknap would be found in the office annex, and pointed the way.

Chief Carvalho went inside, along with his group, leaving the flustered nanny to calm the children, whose protected day had been interrupted by four strangers. He found Belknap's office readily enough, along with Belknap himself, but Belknap, as startled as the nanny, at first sought self-protection behind an official stance.

"I can't have you busting in here like this, officer. Do you realize where you are?"

"No offense meant, Mr. Belknap," the chief said pleasantly. "We're here about a homicide that took place during the past twenty-four hours on presidential property, specifically the Shinnecock lighthouse, which is held in trust by the Denver family. A local lobsterman was found dead in it. You are hardly a suspect, sir, but we have no idea of the correct protocol involved, and we need your help as senior administration official present in liaison with Washington and with the president himself too, of course. And you'll probably want the media off your back, I'm sure, for the moment at least."

Stephanie, completely surprised by the appearance of the law and shocked at hearing it was Farney Gould who had been murdered, sat a silent expectant observer, a hundred questions mulling about in her head. She'd always had a faint fear of the police, seeing them as a sort of heavy-handed authority that you didn't dare resist. Meeting and being friendly with Angi had lessened that feeling slightly, but nevertheless she instantly and for no valid reason felt vaguely guilty of having something to do with the homicide.

Belknap, momentarily placated by the chief's unaggressive demeanor, grabbed his phone, and even while punching buttons on it, snapped at Stephanie, "Nail Mara. Get her in here. Pronto." And then when the phone was answered, "Hank? Bob here. Got a serious problem. Cops found a homicide in the lighthouse. Yes, it's Denver family property. No, I haven't yet told the president. Or anybody else."

For a moment the room was silent until he put back the receiver and said to Chief Carvalho, "That was the chief of staff. You are to ring in the FBI and meanwhile go ahead on your own, with whatever investigation you feel necessary. We'll cooperate with you in any way reasonable that's not injurious to the president or the presidency. But check with me as you go so I can keep Washington minute by minute up to date. I can have my press girl here be a liaison. She's an intern right down the hall. Or Stephanie Crist here, my own intern." He nodded at Stephanie and added, "We'll want to keep complete secrecy from the media, of course. At least until we have more details about security breaches and motive. I mean whether there was any connection to the president or his family being in residence."

A little taken aback by Belknap's officiousness, the chief said, "Miss Crist is already a person of interest in the case, Mr. Belknap. She has twice visited the lighthouse this week and has met the deceased."

"Oh?" Belknap spun his chair toward Stephanie. "You went to town? When was that?"

Stephanie found her voice. "During the meeting, sir. I had time off coming and nothing to do. And I went again some days ago with Mara."

Belknap scowled darkly, as though she'd committed some major offense. "We'll talk about that later. Meanwhile you are to give these officers any assistance they might need."

"Yes, sir." Stephanie was beginning to feel less uncomfortable with the presence of the law and Farney Gould killed than she was disturbed by Belknap. She immediately was certain he would somehow make her pay for taking time off to go to Shinnecock without asking his permission.

Mara appeared as summoned and was ordered to pass the news at once to Alice Fogerty, the president's press secretary back in Washington. Both she and Stephanie were told the police would need to interview them, and for the first time Mara found out who had been murdered, which, given that she'd just seen him a few days ago, alarmed her as much as it did Stephanie. It seemed impossible to her that the lobsterman was dead when he'd been so alive and telling them how he'd lugged the first lady's telescope up to the top of the lighthouse. The news was as frightening as though they'd actually been present when Farney Gould met his end.

The chief of staff, Hank Whittaker, back in

Washington, set in motion the wheels of informing the public in as low-pressure and unpolitical a manner as possible, and the world heard that a man had been ruthlessly murdered on the president's private property with the president in residence only a short distance from the homicide.

Fifteen

Stephanie was right. The deputy chief of staff was indeed troubled by the police appearance and investigation and was hiding something. Or more exactly, hiding a number of things that were faults of his own making.

In his political career, Robert Belknap had learned a vital necessity to success. Besides secrecy in what he was doing as well as in all matters in the Oval Office, it was self-control. It had taken all his ability to appear calm and in command while the police chief and the detectives were in his office with news that left him at once feeling dangerously exposed and renewed all the fears and anxieties he had suffered for some time in Washington long before coming to The Dock.

It also meant acting aggressively to cover his

immediate wave of nervousness, and the moment the police had gone, he turned savagely on Stephanie. "You! Do you realize what you've done?"

To Stephanie, the very accusation that insinuated some dangerous misstep by her exacerbated her unease on learning of the homicide. Her thoughts desperately scrambled to try to remember what wrong, if anything, she was indeed guilty of. For a moment and in the dead silence following Belknap's outburst, she simply stared at him, unable to think, until finally the competitive tennis player in her shot to the surface. Enough was enough, and without thinking, she snapped back indignantly, and in instant rising anger.

"Sir? I haven't done anything wrong. Are you somehow blaming me for someone's murder?" All of Stephanie's long held-down objection and dislike of officialdom and its endless hypocrisy rose up in her like a dark storm. She leaped up, grabbed her handbag from her desk, and headed for the door. "Get yourself another intern."

"Wait." Bullies retreat when challenged. Belknap was no exception. He instantly saw himself in possible trouble with the human relations director back at the White House, or worse, with his own immediate boss, the chief of staff. Stephanie had an excellent work record and was well liked by everyone. Her quitting could cause him damaging embarrassment, and at a very wrong time.

Almost to the door, Stephanie looked back and saw Belknap on his feet and starting toward her.

"I'm sorry, Steph. Didn't mean that. It's just the whole meeting with the bloody Saudis has thrown me for a chop. I could be blamed for the meeting's failure, although I don't see why or how. Please don't go. You're badly needed."

It was so unlike him, so far from the usual boss-employee relationship she shared with him that it stopped Stephanie short, brought her back down to earth, and froze any idea to leave. She managed to find words to bridge her confusion. She said, "I think we both perhaps need a break," and before walking out, put her handbag back down on her desk.

The moment she was gone, Belknap returned weakly to his own desk that he'd left so abruptly, and collapsed into his chair, trying to rediscover his superior status as Stephanie's boss and to overcome embarrassment at the incident.

His outburst had nothing to do with Stephanie. The police visit had unexpectedly ignited all the fears that had constantly followed and nagged at him for months, even years, and now came back to mercilessly haunt him. Except for a constant irritation and jealousy of his wife's close friendship first with the first lady, a woman Belknap profoundly disliked and distrusted, and now with the Lebanese, they were all job-related.

Like many fallible executives, Belknap lived on a razor's edge. He was a man who kept screwing up but who always managed to hide his indiscretions from everyone but himself. His rise to his current powerful position in the government under Whittaker, then the president, was constantly threatened by failures of his own making that he managed painfully to keep hidden.

Over the years that saw his slow rise to power from a prosecuting attorney in the Justice Department, he harbored one stupid and dangerous mistake after another, which he always somehow managed to cover or make seem so insignificant through his lying about them that his career rise had not suffered.

The only person who knew of his errors in judgment, or failures in security, was his wife, Cheryl, in whom he had occasionally confided. She had always brushed aside his confessions as unimportant, but her knowledge of them was more and more worrying.

Belknap's many slips in judgment or security indiscretions, which he successfully had hidden in his first year in the brawl of West Wing politics, had begun with an important top-secret classified memorandum to the president that had ended up in media hands. He alone knew that it had been carelessly left by him in a hotel room, and no fingers had ever been pointed his way.

In his current position in the White House, he then had successfully hidden his role in errors that had caused the Administration embarrassment and were food for its political rivals. And there was always the chance that some such error of judgment on his part would be seen as cause for the recent failure in the negotiations with the Saudis for release of the hostages they held.

And now, of all things, there was a murder on his watch. It was unbearable. And to avoid the nagging misery of it all, he almost fantasized a possible mole in the Administration's midst causing the errors, not him.

Belknap wasn't far off. In reality, there was a mole. And the mole was his wife.

Sixteen

Cheryl Belknap's name on her original birth certificate was Bela Kovacs. Abandoned the same day she was born, she was brought to a public hospital, then placed with foster parents, who were the first to change her name. A successive change was made by Cheryl herself during her final year at high school, along with a new birth certificate, and she picked Cheryl as a first name, copying it from the name of a film star whom at the moment whom she idolized. Her surname, Pennington, that of her second foster parents, she left the same.

Cheryl was not at first a mole in the espionage sense. Stephanie had guessed her character more or less accurately. She was a shallow person who could be called a mole when her entire lifestyle was to burrow into the lives of those higher on the ladder of financial or social success than herself. With her looks and a personality to match, and more than willing to offer any kind of sex to anyone, life to Cheryl, from her earliest school years, had no other moral compass than to use others she saw as more important than herself for her own betterment and to scheme to rise to their level.

In her senior year, she easily made herself desirable to Adrienne Farnsworth, who was influential as class president as well as in the emerging LGBTQ movement and who responded to Cheryl's bisexual orientation. As Adrienne, using her timeless beauty, achieved greater upward success, Cheryl remained attached to her, although limited in public to a normal hug, or even to briefly holding hands in a friendly way. And when Adrienne became first lady, Cheryl soon secured her own way upward by marrying Belknap when he was tagged by the president for a key role in the inner circle of the Oval Office.

When Cheryl met Benji, however, and was smitten by the Lebanese playboy's wealth and celebrity fame, she began to see that her benefit in marriage to Belknap could be lost in an election, and she set her sights on Benji, first with mild flirtation, then with more serious scheming.

Her ambition struck a willing response, for if Cheryl Belknap had little moral compass, Benji, a.k.a. Barijees Alama, had none. Raised in the roiling brawl of Mideast politics in Beirut by a millionaire father who dealt in diamonds, he had, even before his teens, learned that to survive meant adhering to whomever was important in power as well as being prepared constantly to change to another as that power ebbed, and in this way he rose among a myriad of rival and sparring factions.

Skilled in social relations, and using outstanding charm and good looks, the Lebanese established himself with key people in the world of celebrities and finance, along with billionaire oligarch Russians, and quickly discovered those among them who did shady clandestine business in international arms, as well as drugs and human trafficking.

Even before joining her at The Dock, and as he began to realize Cheryl's ambitions, and let her feel more and more a part of his celebrity world, Benji discovered in her a willingness to share classified information gleaned from a husband who foolishly often exposed it to a wife whose confidence he totally trusted. This, along with chance remarks on presidential activities by Adrienne, soon led the Lebanese to find the Summer White House a fertile ground for serious espionage.

Seeing a possible bonanza in the failed secret meeting with the Saudi prince and the U.S. Secretary of State, he had little trouble persuading Cheryl to report verbally on whatever Belknap carelessly left on his desk or around their bedroom that was incriminating, leading her to then take pictures of Belknap's cell phone, in which Belknap had made notes on the meeting and had left on his bedside table while falling asleep after an evening of heavy drinking.

When she was successful, he then told her how to transfer the pictures to an easily hidden thumb drive, and so almost overnight at the Summer White House, the mole, burrowing her way upward socially, became a mole quickly involved in espionage.

At The Dock, however, it became harder and harder for Cheryl to find some place to meet Benji on the sprawling estate that was not under audio and camera surveillance by the Secret Service, or occupied by one of the president's large family, or by staff catering to their needs. Equally difficult for Cheryl was finding a rare moment to enter Belknap's office when the Deputy Chief of Staff or his intern were absent.

Until Cheryl thought of the lighthouse. "Adrienne's had her telescope hauled up top, and what better excuse for meeting than our taking a look through it ourselves," she told Benji in one quickly whispered and laughing moment. And later, in another rare private chance, she said, "And what better place figure how you can get the thumb drive out of here when your visit ends and you'll need to avoid any possible scrutiny by the Secret Service."

Studying her at a formal dinner, dressed in a ravishing Dior gown borrowed from Adrienne and so formally polite and charming, the Lebanese arms dealer could hardly believe that any such seemingly innocent woman could be so quickly and easily corrupted.

Seventeen

P olice Chief Carvalho felt as though he was staring at a blank wall. In ten days, along with the FBI, of interviewing one person after another, not only in Shinnecock but also at The Dock, he'd got nowhere in finding who might have strangled the unfortunate lobsterman, Farney Gould, or even anyone who might have had any motive for doing so. It was as though everyone he'd seen had a Teflon character.

Where the village of Shinnecock was concerned, he'd wasted only a scant amount of time. Neither Shinnecock residents nor tourists were ever reported as getting past the Secret Service barrier at the head of the narrow neck leading to the lighthouse, nor past his own officer, the town cop who was on assignment to keep order in Shinnecock but also to keep anyone from intruding on the lighthouse, which was the private property of the President of the United States.

Quick questioning by his detectives had determined that none who the deceased had dealt with in Barthchester had ever had any personal relations of any kind with him, nor any reason whatsoever to wish him dead and take the serious risk of being accused of homicide. Although the lobsterman's unofficial hometown, his only connection with Barthchester for many past years, other than rightfully claiming it the place of his birth, and where he occasionally ate alone at The Dockside Diner, was delivering his lobster catch to a large commercial company.

In the doughty police chief's judgment then, whomever the guilty party, it could conceivably be someone at The Dock, no matter how impossible that seemed. He had subsequently himself once more gone through interviewing any possible suspect there beginning with household staff and the three nannies. He'd done it cautiously and tactfully, but nonetheless thoroughly and methodically, one by one, while always conscious of treading on presidential property.

"Did you know the lobsterman?"—"Did you ever ride in his boat?"—"Did he give you a secret tour of the lighthouse?"—"Were you ever here before this summer and paid a visit to the lighthouse?"

And as expected, the answers to all questions were negative.

Solely for the record and police protocol, Chief Carvalho had also felt obliged to interview all presidential family members, including the president himself. The meeting with Aaron Denver, held in a little over ten minutes, produced nothing for the chief, other than the experience he would long cherish of speaking personally to the President of the United States. President Denver mercifully had been not only understanding of the chief's obeying police rules in a homicide investigation but gracious in answering directly and to the point any questions put to him.

He experienced the same courtesy as well as the same dead end in questioning the two Denver sons and their wives, along with the Harquist daughter and her husband. None had ever met the lobsterman or even heard of him, and all had ironclad alibis as well.

And then there had been his meeting with the first lady. When he met with her, she came across to the chief as someone who had nothing to offer other than astonishing beauty—she looked thirty, not fifty-seven—and she kept examining her eye makeup during the entire interview, which took place with her sitting at her dressing table in a silk robe that the chief guessed had to have cost close to a thousand.

Even though she had indeed had some connection with the lobsterman in that she had summoned him from the pier, which he passed daily gathering traps, and paid him fifty dollars to take her telescope up to top of the lighthouse, she'd had no further contact with him. The night of the homicide, she had been in the presidential suite with her husband and had him as well as her personal maid to readily prove it.

The same frustration was reached where Summer White House employees were concerned: both a compliant although slightly aggressive Stephanie Crist and a cheerfully academic-looking Mara Harmon, whom the Chief couldn't imagine doing anything more dangerous than reading some scholarly book, had visited the lighthouse and met Farney Gould. His own police officer, Angi Cajun, vouched for Crist. "No way she could be guilty, chief. Had to practically carry her up and down the stair. So shit-terrified of heights, she near passed out on me. She could never do it on her own."

And interviewing Mara Harmon, with whom Crist shared a room, proved equally futile. The press intern had in fact spent most of the time frame in which the coroner said the murder had been committed having coffee and chatting with the two audiovisual technicians of the Summer White House staff, neither of whom had budged from their monitors for one minute as they communicated directly with Washington. Both vouched for her presence all evening as well as she for theirs.

That had left three whom Carvalho had interviewed, though totally skeptical any one of them could be of any help before he had even sat down with them. The first was the deputy chief of staff,

Robert Belknap, who continued to prove difficult, with an Oval Office defensive belligerency in what the chief had instantly seen in every answer to every question as a shield protecting Belknap's high-level position. It was as though the interview was about politics, not the investigation of a homicide.

"I believe the word is 'political hack,'" came laughingly from his intern, Stephanie Crist, when asked to describe his character.

Besides never having even known Farney Gould's name, let alone met the man, Belknap had an ironclad alibi in his wife, who was the second of the final three he interviewed. Cheryl Belknap firmly stated that she had been in bed with her husband watching a favorite late-night political talk show while naming the featured guest speaker along with that of the news anchor, and getting backup confirmation of their viewing from the maid who had brought Belknap his usual late nighttime vodka.

Carvalho couldn't pin down why in his mind he'd felt that everything the woman said in her interview was a lie, only that he felt that lying was part of her very nature. Long experienced at getting information from people, he saw her as having an air about her of not being the woman she wanted to be seen as being.

Reviewing his notes after his talk with her, he realized he had felt that same way in his interview with the first lady. Both, he felt, were hiding something behind a well-known long friendship, but he'd come up with no inkling of what that might be.

Reaching the same dead end with the two Belknaps as he'd reached with all the others he'd interviewed, the police chief turned to the one person left, who, before he even started, he felt would be the most difficult, even though the man apparently had never had any contact with the lobsterman and, like Belknap, professed not even to know who he was.

"I don't mean to sound a snob," the wealthy Lebanese said to the chief with an ingratiating and apologetic smile, "but I'm sure you'll understand that this lobster fellow you say was murdered was not exactly someone in my circle of social acquaintances."

The chief had been told that Barijees Alama, whom everyone called Benji, was a close personal friend of the first lady and her guest at The Dock. But the chief, before he'd even started his interview with him, had a dismal feeling he would be the most impossible witness of all.

Eighteen

Chief Carvalho was to be proven right. With all the other witnesses at The Dock with whom he had spoken, the Chief did some homework first, checking their backgrounds, police records, if any, and running up a rough CV on each if he found enough about them to do so. It was important, he'd learned, to know as much as possible about the person you were interviewing before you asked them a single question. Revealing your knowledge of them as the interview started always threw witnesses off balance and weakened their defense, if they had any.

Given the extreme difficulty that the privileged atmosphere surrounding every aspect of the Summer White House presented—the chief at times felt he was actually trespassing in the Oval

Office—Carvalho came away from all the interviews with the impression that behind a mask of cooperation there lay something unspoken. Long experienced in detective work, he had a feeling that he was perhaps wasting his time interviewing any of them, that somewhere and somehow amidst all the interviews he'd perhaps been close but stonewalled nevertheless.

Barijees Alama was no exception. Beginning with his early years in Lebanon, the police chief found the billionaire Lebanese had attracted the attention of police almost everywhere, but to no avail. As he grew older and better known away from Lebanon, rumors surrounding him began to abound. But even as police scrutiny continued, it failed to produce evidence that the rumors were anything but just that: unproven vague rumors that usually, and more often than not, surround any person of fame. Part of being a celebrity, Carvalho knew, was having an adoring public fantasize a private life that didn't exist.

Accusations of illegal arms sales, of brokering a deal between Havana and a Mexican drug cartel disappeared like a wisp of early morning fog. A report of possible involvement in sex trafficking filed away in England's Scotland Yard alongside that of one of the royal family also proved dead-end worthless. The Barbados police had only an empty file to offer, and in a phone call with the chief constable there, Carvalho heard what a welcome resident Barijees Alama was; how good he was for business on the island, since he spent lavishly and paid a huge docking fee for his enormous yacht when it was in port, which was sometimes months at a time.

And finally, Interpol in Brussels had but three words to say about investigating him, which they had even recently done thoroughly: "Waste of time."

Before his interview with Benji, and although impressed at all the high ranking people the Lebanese knew, including the president and the first lady, Chief Carvalho doggedly persisted in his effort to shine light on the man's past. He'd finally met with Benji himself in the library, and when he did, he'd wasted no time in getting started.

"Sir, you are a guest at The Dock as a friend of the first lady, I believe."

"Of Adrienne, yes."

"May I ask how long you have known her?"

"Quite some time. We met years ago at a gala."

"And where was that?"

"As I remember, it was at Monte Carlo. She was donating her time as a designer model to show off some of the latest from Paris and Milan, with donations going to some charity. I can't remember which, but an important one, perhaps Save the Children."

"You've been seen here constantly in her presence along with her friend Cheryl Belknap."

"Yes, I believe they've been close friends since school."

"And how long have you known Mrs. Belknap?"

"Cheryl? Only here this summer, really. In the past I've run across her from time to time, although very briefly. At dinners or functions of some kind, that sort of thing."

"When did you first meet Farney Gould?"

"I'm sorry. Who?"

"Farney Gould." Pause, when Benji looked blank. then, "The lobsterman."

"Oh, of course. The murdered person, right?"

It went like that for a full thirty minutes with Benji, friendly politeness itself, seeming more than eager to honestly answer every question put to him and to want to be helpful. The lighthouse? He'd heard all about it, and of course seen it from the lawn at The Dock. One could hardly miss it. But no, he'd never visited it or had any desire to do so.

"Why the first lady ever wanted the telescope up there," he said, "without checking if she could see through the windows, is a mystery. I'm told that they are so dirty from years of salt spray you can hardly see through them."

The secret meeting with the Saudi emissary? "I'm afraid I can't tell you anything about that," Benji said. "Like everybody else, even the first lady, I was cordoned off, and I could only see the various people from a distance."

"You weren't at the reception?"

"The reception? Yes, of course, and I did speak for a few minutes with the Saudi prince. It turned out that I had played golf with him several years ago at Riyadh when I went there for a Formula 1 race event. I owned one of the racing teams."

His answer to the key question of where he had been between midnight and two in the morning, the time frame of the homicide, was as utterly guileless as all his other answers, perhaps even more so. "Oh. I was sound asleep, of course. It's close to impossible to do anything else here of an evening, what with all the Secret Service wandering about everywhere, except to drink and watch television in the living room with the ladies, which I did until it got very late and they went off to bed."

And so there it was, the Police Chief thought. *One more dead end.* In spite of himself, he had to admit that he'd found his time with the international billionaire celebrity interestingly amenable. Most celebrities, Carvalho knew, more often than not defensively wrapped their true being in the disguise of friendly and open frankness, the way the Lebanese celebrity did. The man had expressed amusement at all of the rumors that the chief questioned and that had for years swirled around him. He had even added a couple the chief had not uncovered. But to all extent and purpose, even if he felt Benji might be hiding something, the Lebanese had been cleared of any fingerprint- or DNA-connected guilt when the first lady said he'd once handled her telescope, nor had his prints been found anywhere in the lighthouse.

Like everyone else, Benji had to be reluctantly eliminated as a suspect.

Nineteen

Carvalho gave up. His own detectives, along with the state forensic unit and the FBI, had only managed an educated guess that Farney Gould had possibly interrupted a robbery of the expensive amateur telescope that he had earlier taken up to the top of the lighthouse at the request of the first lady. But who might have been trying to steal the telescope remained a stubbornly unanswered question. Every person in the village of Shinnecock who could possibly have got by troopers or the Secret Service guarding the causeway to the lighthouse was checked and proved innocent.

And summing up his interviews with all at The Dock, including everyone with the Summer White House, he'd found not only no one there either who had any conceivable reason for killing the lowly lobsterman, but that most didn't even know who he was.

Farney Gould, the weary police chief concluded, would not be missed for long. He was not the president, nor any person of lesser importance, and there were others among lobstermen who would gladly take over the lush lobstering in the waters above the dangerous shelf presided over by Shinnecock's once active lighthouse. With the FBI drawing the same empty-handed conclusions that he had, and expressing less and less interest, the chief felt that any continued investigation was wasting time and money. To continue meant exhausting all the resources of his small police force, whose main responsibility was to Barthchester, a far larger place than Shinnecock.

"I think," Carvalho said, speaking a day after interviewing Benji to those of his officers concerned, including Officer Cajun, to whom he'd assigned the Shinnecock police duty, "that we have to call off any further investigation of the Shinnecock homicide as an expensive waste of time. So it's back to more essential work right here in Barthchester for everybody."

And then, thinking to inject the meeting with lightheartedness and not meaning to be disdainful, he added jokingly, "That includes you, Officer Cajun. Forget the homicide and resume your occasional duties in Shinnecock with whatever duties that your 'Town Cop' label applies to, and if not interrupting sleep."

His words provoked a scattered titter, and even one guffaw, from a few officers who saw Angi's assignment as a laugh and a way to avoid work.

Angi, however, didn't think his signaling her out was funny. She took the chief's words literally, and not the way he'd actually meant as a compliment expressed in a jocular negative way, and they rankled deeply.

She almost immediately felt humiliated, with all the work she did keeping Shinnecock within the bounds of law and order, and been so proud of, as utterly meaningless. Without speaking to anyone, she left Barthchester and went back to Shinnecock where, entering the little office she shared with Charley How, she threw herself into her chair without answering when Charley asked how the meeting went.

It was only with effort, and only because of who Charley was, that she finally managed to speak. "It went lousy. He called off any further homicide investigation and made all the guys laugh at my being the town cop. Like, how low can you get."

Charley kept his silence until, after a few minutes, Angi rose to sling her utility belt around her hips. He'd quickly seen how troubled she was, and guessing why, he inwardly cursed Carvalho's seeming insensitivity.

He said, casually, "Where are you off to, kid?"

"To work," Angi said sullenly. "I'm the fucking town cop, remember?"

"Remember? Yeah, I do," Charley said. And

then he added, "Just like everyone else in this town who likes you and respects you, and with all the kids seeing you as their hero. Don't give a flying shit what Carvalho or any Barthchester cop says. To everyone here, this old NYPD relic included, you're someone who makes Shinnecock the good place it is."

Angi didn't answer, and out on Main Street, stood silently amidst a usual first-in-the-day swirl of tourists, and staring at nothing in particular for a long moment, except perhaps seeing the not very distant Shinnecock lighthouse. Something had just happened to her.

She felt suddenly different, and a defiance surged up in her. Old Charley was right. Fuck Carvalho and all the guys in Barthchester. They weren't here in Shinnecock. They didn't know the first thing about how important policing was in this village, or how much work. Let any one of them spend one day with her being the town cop they thought so funny and they'd soon quit laughing.

She was thinking that way, feeling the sudden change in her because of how old Charley saw her job, and who, she thought, was better qualified to judge than him, when she became more aware of staring at the lighthouse. All thoughts of failure were replaced by thoughts about the unsolved homicide. She had been about to tell Carvalho one such thought she'd had when he'd shut down any further discussion.

As soon as she could, she was damned well

going back up to the top of the old lighthouse and have another look around, Angi told herself, before heading quickly down toward the causeway to help a trooper trying to stop a tourist from going to gawk at where Farney Gould had died.

Twenty

Three days before Angi's renewed determination, after the police chief had finished interviewing him and evening pleasantries were over, and with good-nights said to the first lady and several of her children, Benji retired to the library of The Dock, fixed himself a drink, and dropped into a comfortable chair. Unknown to Chief Carvalho, his interview had produced results that he could hardly have even imagined. It had been only with enormous effort that Benji had somehow controlled himself and kept hidden from Carvalho behind seemingly casual pleasantries, the nightmare of truth that could ruin his life.

But now, with the police chief mercifully gone and his suspicions suppressed, everything in the past week came back to the Lebanese in a rush, beginning with Cheryl's success in obtaining cell phone information on the highly secret meeting with the Saudis and getting it all on a thumb drive.

Every living moment had been one of fear and anxiety since she had then ruined that first success in casually saying the day after, and when they were briefly alone together, "I was with Adrienne in her room. The telescope was out on her bed, and she was in the shower, leaving me alone with it. The thumb drive felt like it was burning a hole in my pocket, and making me unbearably nervous, and I suddenly thought what a great place to hide it until I could give it to you. So I just unscrewed the big lens at the end of the telescope and dropped it into the scope's insides.

"If Adrienne found it before I could get it out again, I could always tell her it was porn photos I'd collected for Robert, who is into porn in a big way, the stupid ass. I had no idea that Adrienne was planning to have the telescope taken up to the lighthouse that very day. Away from all the prying eyes in this damned place, she told me."

Cheryl had hardly stopped talking, with every word she spoke like an unexpected and violent blow, when he had cursed himself for getting involved with a woman so stupid. He still remembered try-ing not to let her see the jolt he'd felt to his entire system not just because of the possible ruination of everything he'd seen for himself and his future in what she'd stolen from her husband's phone, but in the very real danger she'd put him in as well.

He'd wanted to use the information on the meeting with the Saudis that she'd gleaned to coerce the Saudis into giving him something of greater value than money: the prestige and power of eventually controlling all of the sports events at Riyadh that the Saudis were so eager to promote: Formula 1 racing, golf, football, tennis, even one day the Olympics. And he had planned to safely take care of the thumb drive by simply mailing it to himself at his New York apartment to avoid customs inspection if mailed to the Barbados or Paris. But now?

If Adrienne didn't use the telescope, the thumb drive's presence could be spotted by the Secret Service when she returned with it to Washington. Routine checks were always made on any baggage coming into the White House, even the president's, to make sure nobody was unwittingly bringing in an explosive. His own baggage had been carefully scrutinized when he came to The Dock.

If that were to happen, and the first lady certainly seen only as an unwitting mule, the finger of guilt, what with all the endless rumored criminal incidents in his past, would surely be pointed at him first of all. He might possibly survive an investigation and the unwanted glare of media attention—he always had—but at what cost? One way or another, Cheryl's utter stupidity would have to be eliminated. If not, there'd be a complete disruption of his life as well as the loss of the thumb-drive information and all it could mean to him.

In the wracking darkness that flooded Benjie's mind, there'd been one faint ray of hope. The thumb drive had almost certainly been missed by the police forensic unit, who'd had no reason to take the big lens off the telescope, and he couldn't take the chance of the police returning the telescope itself to the first lady and her then possessively locking the telescope away someplace he couldn't reach prior to her return to Washington and the White House. Like it or not, he'd realized, he'd had to get it. His own life could possibly depend on it. He'd had no other choice.

He'd thought of driving all the way around to park someplace in the village, then had dismissed the idea. A car in the dead of night when nothing else stirred would surely attract Secret Service attention. He had discarded as well the thought of walking along the shore and exposing himself to the Coast Guard patrol boat lolling right off the pier. So, he had ended up using the well-guarded path to Shinnecock and the protection of darkness it offered.

With the village in middle-of-the-night complete silence, he'd somehow managed to slip, unseen or heard, past a Secret Service watch, the agent off guard due to the hour. He'd left the path short of it being blocked, and had carefully got over the rocky shore into the sea. Silently swimming the few yards to the causeway to the lighthouse, he'd slipped past the lobsterman, who, since the night was warm, was asleep in his boat moored to one of the massive rocks at the lighthouse base.

Finding the lighthouse door locked but certain the key had to be somewhere close, he'd made a fumbling search for it, one made difficult because of the gloves he'd worn to avoid leaving any prints, in case, for some reason he couldn't imagine, they would be found.

He'd finally got the key from where it was hidden behind the half-open inscribed bronze plaque affixed to the lighthouse wall, and he'd silently opened the door, and felt his way up the spiral staircase.

He remembered all that; he remembered climbing endlessly upward using his phone light to see, then getting through the thankfully open trapdoor and finding himself at the top of the lighthouse.

Now, fixing another drink in the silence of the household around him, he remembered the equal silence up there, his surprise and instant wariness of the massive machinery occupying much of its space, his near panic in wondering where the telescope might be, and his relief in discovering it lying close by on the floor.

He'd taken off the lens cover and unscrewed the big lens of the telescope, and found the little thumb drive, and put it in his pocket. It was there now, where he still kept it until he could get to a post office. Then he'd screwed the lens back on, and he remembered his flood of relief when he did, then his starting back to the trapdoor.

He remembered it all until the unexpected violent blow that sent him crashing into the rusty mass of the old iron machinery and his terrible struggle in the darkness.

Sitting in the quiet library, the house asleep around him, his mind was filled with a jumble of all-at-once confusion; there'd been awareness of someone else, the strong smell of liquor and fish and unwashed body sweat, his struggle to free himself from hands that were like iron; there'd been that hoarse shout, "Hold on, you. You ain't stealing nothing, mister," and then being held helpless as both he and his attacker were caught by the invisible gears of the ancient machinery they'd fallen against that suddenly came alive and moved, grinding slowly around.

He remembered the strangled gasps of his attacker and himself finally tearing loose and falling back from the gears as they continued to drag his still trapped attacker until they stopped and he too fell away.

After that, everything was darkness and silence; he remembered nothing more until he found himself down at the foot of the lighthouse and cautiously regaining the path back to The Dock. And his near panicked fear ever since, especially when being interviewed, that he might have somehow left behind evidence on the man he'd struggled with. Had that been himself who pushed the inert dead body through the open trapdoor to look like the man had died from the fall? And then walked over the body at the bottom of the stair? It must have been.

He tried to remember, and some of it came back vaguely. And afterward, he remembered almost nothing except somehow getting back to his guest room at The Dock, and taking off his clothes, and when finally in bed, staring blankly at his sports jacket, where it had been torn in his breaking loose from the gears after his violent fall against them. The jacket was filthy with grease and rust, and he tossed it in a laundry basket to be sent to the dry cleaner.

And now, slumped again deep in the library chair with his drink, he tried to shut off any further memories of the terror at what he'd been through, while at the same time feeling a growing flood of relief. It was all over. He had the thumb drive, the future it could give him, and safety. He'd done it and got away with it.

Twenty-One

Except he hadn't.

The wheels of justice grind slowly, but they grind nevertheless, and more often than not in completely unexpected ways.

Charley How had a message for Angi when she came to work the day after he'd tried to cheer her up and apparently had succeeded.

"Got a call from the chief," he said. "Somebody speaking for the first lady called him. She told him the first lady wanted her telescope brought back to The Dock, and right away."

Inwardly, Angi cursed. It was a particularly busy tourist time, and while determined to get to the lighthouse to give more thought to Farney Gould's untimely death, she hadn't counted on mixing it up with lugging the telescope all the way to The Dock. She'd be kept busy doing it for at least an hour, probably more, and it would prevent her from policing the tourists from getting out of hand nearly everywhere.

Angi was hardened to death, but nevertheless, after getting to the lighthouse, she felt a slight chill in her spine when she opened the heavy door and went to the foot of the spiral stair. The last time she'd been there, she'd found Farney Gould lying dead, limbs twisted every way, his head cracked open like an eggshell, and a lot of blood around. Farney wasn't someone she particularly liked, but he'd been a village institution, and she'd got to a state of familiarity with him in which he was simply a part of her daily life. His murder had troubled her more than she would have been troubled by the homicide of most people.

Reaching the top of the stair and getting through the trap door onto the steel-plated floor surrounding the light mechanism, she saw the telescope at once. She picked it up. It wasn't as heavy as she'd expected, and she had started back to the trap door and the stair with it when she stopped short, thinking.

She had almost unconsciously noticed something peculiar about the turntable and the ancient iron gears below it that once had rotated the mirror platform around the center kerosene lamp to send bright reflected warning light out through the surrounding windows. She realized she didn't see either the lever that activated the heavy mechanism and started the cable to unwind off the drum, or the hand crank that laboriously wound the cable back up.

Odd, she thought. The machine must have been run. But by whom? By Forensic or by the two detectives who'd come up? She didn't think so. When she'd spoken to them, none had mentioned the machinery at all. One of them, at least, surely would have said so if they had.

She put down the telescope, and going around the heavy mass of clockwork-like gears, soon found the operating lever. Out of sight from the trap door to the stair and from where the telescope had lain, it was stuck down, in the "on" position. Angi lifted it up and pushed it down again. Nothing happened. The mechanism had indeed been used, but barely a foot or more of cable had unwound from the cable drum. It had either jammed for some reason or somehow had finally just given up on life.

Asking herself again why the machinery had been started and by whom, Angi remembered that the detectives had determined there'd been a struggle in a possibly interrupted robbery, and perhaps in such a struggle, someone had fallen against the lever, starting the gears to turn and old drum to unwind its cable.

She looked at the double row of gears more closely and saw that several large rusty teeth of one gear had broken off. Thinking that this could have been the cause of the machinery stopping, she put her head in amongst the gears to check and saw, way back almost out of sight and barely distinguishable from the jammed gears themselves, the dried rust-colored blood that stained one tiny link of a necklace, which she recognized as being similar to the broken chain embedded in the neck of Farney Gould.

Something like an electric shock ran through Angi. The necklace he wore, she realized, must have been seized by the gears, strangling him, and as the machine began its circular path, slowly dragged him along to his death, holding him fast until it had been jammed to a stop by its own broken gear teeth. Forensic had missed it because of their lack of familiarity with the lighthouse light mechanism. It was only someone like her who could realize that the machinery had been used and, wondering why, investigate it fully when going around to its unseen side.

Feeling as though she were actually there when Farney met his death, she took a deep breath and got out her phone. Using its light to look even deeper into the rusty gears, she noticed something else even farther back amongst them than the necklace link she'd seen, and which she knew at once didn't belong there. It was a barely visible thread.

Angi made no claims to be anything of a forensic expert, but looking more closely at the thread after she'd carefully removed it, she knew it had either been blown like dust into the gears by some faint draft of wind, or, she suspected, since it appeared new, it had more than likely been torn from the clothing of someone. Forensic experts could most likely determine something from it. They perhaps could even identify what kind of clothing, and that in turn could possibly lead to whom it belonged. It didn't look to her the same color as any of Farney Gould's rarely washed dark clothing. It was beige and looked like silk.

When, mid-morning, Police Chief Mike Carvalho answered his phone, it was to hear the caller say, "Chief, Angi Cajun. I'm up at the top of the lighthouse. Came to take back the telescope to the first lady."

A brief pause, and then, "Sir, about the homicide here. I think I've found something that possibly could lead Forensic to someone involved."

Twenty-Two

The police did of course follow the lead given them, and it didn't take long for forensic experts with both the FBI and Interpol to determine the origin of the tiny thread found by the Shinnecock police officer. It was traced to an expensive fabric, and then to a specific manufacturer, who revealed that a very limited number of rolls of it had been made.

These in turn were sold to a handful of bespoke tailors, who then made light sports jackets from it for only a limited number of wealthy clients, each jacket specifically fitted.

An arrest soon followed, and the public then endlessly saw Barijees Alama in handcuffs, legs shackled and surrounded by police, on television and in newspapers and talked about everywhere as involved in a murder dangerously close to the president, and what's more, and perhaps most shockingly, a once intimate friend of the first lady.

Where is that first lady now, and where are all those other people who were present at The Dock during that alarming summer when a last-ditch attempt to free Saudi hostages soured the United States in its relations with the Arab kingdom?

With the president no longer occupying the White House and involved with a foundation overseeing several major charities in Africa, the first lady, between unwanted appearance at fund-raisers, continues to find solace and refuge from reality in her telescope.

Their tennis playing daughter, too old for the pro singles circuit, has found moderate professional success playing doubles. The deputy chief of staff, Robert Belknap, has found a job with a Wall Street law firm which, ignoring his alcoholism, uses his name and former job to gain new clients.

His wife, Cheryl, is enjoying that Benji never ratted on her, only because in doing so he would have further pointed a finger of espionage at himself and added years to his maximum eleven-year prison sentence for involuntary manslaughter. Plotting a divorce, Cheryl has managed to hook onto a major Hollywood film producer notoriously suspected of abusing underage women, some of whom, it is rumored, she introduced to him to gain favor for herself.

Stephanie Crist and Mara Harmon? With their remaining close friends, Mara has settled into a job as a prestigious writer with *The Atlantic,* and Stephanie is a respected political columnist with ProPublica.

Which leaves us Angi. The town cop, as she was known for a few years when she policed the village of Shinnecock, has been rewarded by a grateful police chief before his retirement with a position of detective at Barthchester. A notable increase in salary and, according to fellow officers, one day seeing herself as chief, has come with the promotion, enabling her to buy her mother a new two-bedroom home, which they share.

Hanging on a wall in a prominent place is the coveted police award for distinction in the line of duty. Next to it is a picture of the famed Shinnecock lighthouse, which, as one juror stated during the trial of the Lebanese celebrity, bore the actual guilt for the murder of a lowly lobsterman to add to the many alternative stories of lives it saved with its slowly revolving lights warning mariners of the deadly underwater shelf of rock it stood guard over.

End

About the Author

David Osborn, for over sixty years a writer, lives in Connecticut with his wife, a once American and European ballerina, then renowned in international health policy. Their daughter, a PhD psychologist, practices in Sydney, Australia. Their lawyer son is an advocate for the welfare of animals worldwide.

Novels and Screenwriting

Novels

The Glass Tower – Hodder & Stoughton
Open Season – The Dial Press
The French Decision – Doubleday
Love and Treason – New American Library
Heads – Bantam
Murder on Martha's Vineyard – Lynx
Murder on the Chesapeake – Simon & Schuster
Murder in the Napa Valley – Simon & Schuster
The Last Pope – Source Books
The Cape Cod Blue – Dagmar Miura
Alicia's Secret (young adult) – Dagmar Miura
A Cold Wind from the Andes – Dagmar Miura
The Head Hunters – Dagmar Miura
Looking Back: The Long Life of a Writer (a memoir)
Delta Red – Dagmar Miura
Eventide – Dagmar Miura
The Somersville Bodies – Dagmar Miura
Cold Case 369 – Dagmar Miura
The Lighthouse (a novella)– Dagmar Miura

For Children

Jessica and the Crocodile Knight (a novel) – HarperCollins

Jessica and Her Adventures in Fairyland (collection of five novellas) – Dagmar Miura

Ophelia and Her Forest Friends (series of ten stories) – Dagmar Miura

Jessica and the Witch's Broom – Dagmar Miura

Jessica and the Flying Unicorns – Dagmar Miura

Jessica and the Golden Swan Feather – Dagmar Miura

Feature Films

The Trap (original story and screenplay; Academy Award nominee for Best Foreign Film) – Columbia

Open Season (screenplay, adapted from Osborn's own best-selling novel *Open Season*) – Columbia

Chase a Crooked Shadow (original story and screenplay co-written with Charles Sinclair; listed by the British Academy of Motion Picture Science as "One of the ten best suspense scripts ever written") – Warner Bros.

Moment of Danger, a.k.a. *Malaga* (screenplay adapted from the novel) – Warner Bros.

Malaga (screenplay) – Warner Bros.

Maroc 7 (original story and screenplay) – J. Arthur Rank

Deadlier Than the Male (original story and screenplay) – J. Arthur Rank

Some Girls Do (original story and screenplay) – J. Arthur Rank

The Road to Dusty Death (screenplay) – J. Arthur Rank

The Games (screenplay) – Associated British

Follow the Boys (original story and screenplay) – MGM

Beat Girl (original story and screenplay) – Renown Films/British Lion

Stop-over Forever (original story and screenplay) – British Lion

Winter Holiday (original story and screenplay) – MGM

Penny Gold (original story and screenplay) – J. Arthur Rank/Columbia

Whoever Slew Auntie Roo? (original story and screenplay) – Paramount & American International

Murder, She Said (screenplay, Agatha Christie adaptation) – MGM

Murder at the Gallop (screenplay, Agatha Christie adaptation) – MGM

Feature-length Documentaries

Fangio, The History of Formula One Racing (original screenplay; executive producer) – Volpi Productions

Why Ireland – Irish Tourist Bureau

Films Canceled While in Production

HMS Ulysses – Volpi Productions (screenplay adaptation of the Alistair MacLean novel about protecting North Sea convoys to Russia during World War II; production halted when a key warship was unavailable)

The Mad Motorists – Volpi Productions (screenplay adaptation from the Allen Andrews novel about the 1907 Peking to Paris race)

Eagle at Sundown – Dragon Films (original screen story about Napoleon's escape from Elba; starring Douglas Fairbanks; in production when canceled)

Les Petits Rats – Disney (original story and screenplay about the Paris Ballet school; production begun, then canceled)

Hunters' Horn – McCahon Productions (screenplay adaptation from the Harriette Simpson Arnow novel; production canceled; financing failure)

Blood on the Rose – British Lion (screenplay adaptation from the Phyllis Hastings novel)

Television

Bouquet for Miss Olive (three-act play; British Television Producers Association nominee for Best Play of the Year) – Granada/ITV

Three on a Gas Ring (three-act play; British Television Producers Association nominee for Best Play of the Year) – Granada/ITV

Why George Brown Hanged (three-act play) –
    Granada/ITV

Arthur of the Britons (pilot and three scripts on the
    life of King Arthur; Writers Guild of Great
    Britain award winner for Best British Children's
    Series)

The Antiquers (original story, pilot, and six episodes
    in the sitcom series) – Irish National Television

www.ingramcontent.com/pod-product-compliance
Lightning Source LLC
Chambersburg PA
CBHW040539170726
48295CB00012B/527